T0384356

# STAY
# DEAD

# STAY
# DEAD

## APRIL HENRY

Christy Ottaviano Books
LITTLE, BROWN AND COMPANY
New York Boston

Copyright © 2024 by April Henry

Cover image of blood spatter © hareluya/Shutterstock.com; grunge texture © Nik Merkulov/Shutterstock.com; black boot © SENIMANTO_ID/Shutterstock.com. Cover design by Neil Swaab. Cover copyright © 2024 by Hachette Book Group, Inc. Interior design by Michelle Gengaro-Kokmen.

Christy Ottaviano Books
Hachette Book Group
1290 Avenue of the Americas, New York, NY 10104
Visit us at LBYR.com

First Edition: May 2024

Christy Ottaviano Books is an imprint of Little, Brown and Company. The Christy Ottaviano Books name and logo are trademarks of Hachette Book Group, Inc.

Image of snowcapped mountains © Awana JF/Shutterstock.com; snowy landscape © Pavels/Shutterstock.com; frozen lake © Standret/Shutterstock.com; road with thunderclouds © Dudarev Mikhail/Shutterstock.com.

Little, Brown and Company books may be purchased in bulk for business, educational, or promotional use. For information, please contact your local bookseller or the Hachette Book Group Special Markets Department at special.markets@hbgusa.com.

Library of Congress Cataloging-in-Publication Data
Names: Henry, April, author.
Title: Stay dead / April Henry.
Description: New York : Little, Brown and Company, 2024. | Audience: Ages 12–18. | Summary: Entrusted with a key by her dying mother, sixteen-year-old Milan pretends she perished along with her mother as she navigates freezing conditions, outsmarts assassins, and unravels a deadly conspiracy to save herself and others.
Identifiers: LCCN 2023035250 | ISBN 9780316480291 (hardcover) | ISBN 9780316480499 (ebook)
Subjects: CYAC: Mystery and detective stories. | Conspiracies—Fiction. | Survival—Fiction. | Murder—Fiction. | LCGFT: Detective and mystery fiction.
Classification: LCC PZ7.H39356 St 2024 | DDC [Fic]—dc23
LC record available at https://lccn.loc.gov/2023035250

ISBNs: 978-0-316-48029-1 (hardcover), 978-0-316-48049-9 (ebook)

Printed in Indiana, USA

LSC-C, 04/25

Printing 2, 2025

For Nancy Husbands,
in appreciation of the thousands of
nature walks we have taken

# Chapter 1

## MILAN
# FLAILING. FAILING. FALLING.

MILAN SLUMPED, TRYING TO TELEGRAPH THAT SHE DIDN'T CARE. Her stomach ached.

Behind her polished oak desk, Ms. Robbins steepled her hands, matching fingertip to fingertip.

Milan made herself meet the headmistress's cool gray gaze. The silence stretched out until it was nearly unbearable.

It was Ms. Robbins who finally broke. "I know this last year has been difficult for you."

*Difficult?* Milan suppressed a bark of laughter.

"Still, I would have expected better from the daughter of a senator." Ms. Robbins separated her hands and laid them on her desk. "Of two senators."

"Not simultaneously." Milan's voice was flat. "My dad had to die for my mom to get his seat."

Ms. Robbins winced. "I'm sure the circumstances were incredibly difficult for both of you, but she is carrying on your dad's legacy of protecting the environment." Before becoming a senator, Milan's dad had been the CEO of Earth Energy, an alternative energy company that harvested energy from the wind, the sun, and even the ocean's waves. As a senator, he'd hoped to do even more to reverse the damage humans had done.

Her mom, who shared the same focus, had liked Briar Woods' green campus, which included low-flow toilets, environmental restoration projects, and growing their own organic food.

Before her dad died, Milan had attended public school in Portland. Her mom had worked part-time for Save Our Salmon, roping in their deep-pocketed friends for boring fundraisers. Most weekends, her dad flew home. He and Milan would go out for breakfast or on long hikes.

The morning he died, her dad had been driving Milan to their favorite waffle place when his SUV drifted out of the lane. The resulting accident flipped their RAV4 Hybrid over and over. Her dad died instantly, and Milan's left leg was now held together with pins.

After her mom ran for his seat and won, Milan braced for the move from Portland to DC, for leaving behind Chance and all her other friends. The reality was worse.

According to her mom, the public schools in DC were notorious for metal detectors, high dropout rates, and low test scores. But putting Milan in one of DC's private schools would have looked elitist. Her mom didn't want to be seen as privileged or as someone who thought her kid deserved better, even though she was and she did.

So citing a senator's long hours and her new status as a single parent, her mom enrolled Milan in a Massachusetts boarding school landscaped with native plants and powered by several acres of solar panels. In her mom's eyes, it was the perfect solution. Milan would get a good education and be supervised 24-7.

Perfect, that is, for everyone but Milan. She had felt like an orphan. She was homesick all the time. Ever since, she had been flailing. Failing. Falling. This boarding school in Colorado was her third in six months.

The first school had been filled with rich kids, many the children of politicians, who planned to attend Harvard or Stanford. Milan had broken into the calculus teacher's office, photographed upcoming tests, and sold them. Not for the money. She just wanted to reveal the other kids for the phonies they were.

Boarding school number two was girls only, complete with ridiculous plaid outfits, wilderness trips, and twice-daily mandated chapel, where they were reminded they were stewards of the earth. Remembering it now, Milan touched the tattoo inside her left wrist, the homemade one that had gotten her expelled. When a teacher noticed the bandage under the cuff of her white blouse, he'd worried it was hiding a suicide attempt.

But when Milan was forced to expose her tender pale skin, there were no cuts. Just four black letters and a question mark—*WWJD?*—each outlined by swollen red skin. (It might not have been the best idea to watch YouTube videos and then give yourself what was basically a prison tattoo with a sewing needle and ballpoint pen ink.)

It had hurt to make all those tiny holes, but Milan had bit down on a wooden chopstick and not made a sound. The pain had actually been a bonus. It pushed every thought from her head. Made her forget what had happened. Even though that was why she made the tattoo in the first place.

Thinking *WWJD?* stood for "What Would Jesus Do?," the school almost let her stay. But the *J* was really for "Jack," her dad, who had set his sights on the presidency. Who had wanted to be like that earlier Jack, Jack Kennedy.

Instead her dad was dead. And it was her fault.

Ms. Robbins's sigh interrupted Milan's thoughts. "I was hoping you'd learned some lessons from your previous experiences. Your mother said you had." Her mom had been so sure Briar Woods Academy would be right for her. Not just for the environmental focus, but also because everyone here was troubled. Broken in some way. Just like her. "What were you thinking, Milan?" Her voice was kind.

What had Milan been thinking? She wasn't too sure herself. It had started with her impatience at the literature teacher, who only assigned books by old dead white guys. Who was basically an old dead white guy himself. Who rolled his eyes when she brought up Colson Whitehead, Celeste Ng, and Jesmyn Ward. Two days ago, he had banished her to the hall after she asked if he'd assigned *Moby Dick* just to kill everyone's desire to read.

She was supposed to have sat at an old wooden desk and reflected on her behavior. Milan hadn't even hidden her phone in her bra, so she had nothing to entertain her.

Nothing, that is, except for her lighter. At this school, just like in a prison, cigarettes were currency, furtively smoked by every bad girl worth her salt. Milan had even persuaded Chance to send her two packs inside a hollowed-out book, along with a bunch of real books the school's library didn't have on its dusty shelves.

Slouched in the chair, Milan had flicked the lighter on and off, on and off, hating it here. Hating herself. After noticing a loose thread hanging from her shirt, she snapped it off and offered it to the flame. In a blink, it flared then disappeared. What else could she burn? A crumpled sticky note from her backpack caught for a brief second. When it singed her fingers, she blew it out.

Was there anything else she could light and then extinguish? Her eyes fell on the book that had basically gotten her kicked out of class. She opened to a random page.

*"In connection with this appellative of 'Whalebone whales,' it is of great importance to mention, that however such a nomenclature may be convenient in facilitating allusions to some kind of whales . . ."*

No wonder no one at this school liked to read! She slammed the book shut.

As if they belonged to someone else, Milan watched her fingers flick the lighter's wheel and then apply the flame to a corner of the yellowed pages. Her cheeks were puffed full of air, ready to blow it out. But instead of a lick of flame, the fire became a whole open hungry mouth. The book became a bonfire. When Milan shrieked and jumped to her feet, it fell. Suddenly the carpet too was alight.

After that, things were a blur. The air filling with choking gray smoke. The deafening wail of the fire alarm. The literature teacher appearing with a fire extinguisher as Milan's classmates evacuated. The automatic sprinklers suddenly plastering her clothes and hair to her skin.

Now, sitting in Ms. Robbin's office, Milan felt stupid and ashamed. Her father would definitely never have done that.

"I didn't mean for it to happen." Her voice shook, giving her away. She dug her fingernails into her palms.

"I'm guessing you didn't," Ms. Robbins said. "Personally, I like you, Milan. There's a spark inside you." She bit her lip. "Sorry. Poor choice of words. But I'm afraid the board has overruled me."

Where would Milan end up now? Did they have military schools for girls?

"I have informed your mother she has to come get you immediately. Well, actually, I told your mother's personal assistant."

Jenna Spencer. Milan could just imagine the face she'd made. Jenna was only eight years older than her but acted like she was a full-fledged adult and Milan a first grader. Too bad Ms. Robbins hadn't reached Eric Scott, formerly her dad's chief of staff and now her mom's. He was good at fixing things that seemed unfixable.

"You're making Mom come all the way out to Colorado from DC?" The last two schools had just stuck Milan on a commercial flight. Milan's family had their own plane, though when people called it a jet, she always corrected them. It was a turboprop, not a jet, so it was more fuel efficient. It also didn't sound so annoyingly rich, even though it was basically what people thought of when they said "jet." Wide pale leather seats. Plenty of space. No need to go through security. And it had cost millions.

Ms. Robbins nodded. "She was already planning to fly to Portland for a meeting. Now she'll be detouring here to pick you up first."

Portland. Milan's heart lifted. She could go home. Even just for a day or two. She could see Chance and her other old friends. Maybe even figure out some way to stay.

# Chapter 2

# JANIE
# SEE HER CRY

**Three years earlier**

THROUGH THE MESH OF THE SCREEN DOOR, JANIE REGARDED THE man who had just rung her doorbell. She hooked her fingers through Rocky's collar. Rocky was growling, but then again, he never liked strangers.

The man, who was about her daughter Becca's age, stood on Janie's sagging porch. His Timberlands looked like he had just pulled them out of the box. Behind him was a shiny maroon Chevy pickup. The road to the farm hadn't seen tires that new for a long, long time.

"Can I help you?" Janie asked. She had her hair pulled back in a ponytail, and she was wearing sweatpants, an old sweatshirt with the University of Ohio logo on it, and socks with no shoes. Her feet were starting to get cold. It had been a long day. She'd been up since four.

"Beautiful piece of land you got here," he said, turning to wave his arm.

Janie knew what she had. Not much. The gutters were falling off the house, the dairy barn was listing, and the fields where their seventy-nine cows grazed barely grew enough fescue and clover. Still, it supported her, Becca, Becca's husband, Thad, and the two grandkids, Noelle and Darcy.

For half her adult life, Janie had run this farm, doing the work of three men with the help of strong coffee and a tractor with an engine that required constant tinkering. On a farm there was no such thing as paid vacation, no matching 401(k), no sleeping in on weekends. Success was measured not in profits, but in years without a loss. And even that depended on so many things that Janie couldn't control.

Most years she barely made enough to keep up with the taxes and loans, but it was still Janie's farm, her family's, and she knew it, every cow, every tree, every patch of rye and orchard grass.

Janie would be damned if she was the generation that lost the farm. And she'd be damned if she'd let this stranger see her cry. "I'm not looking to sell." She started to close the door.

The man raised his hand, palm facing her, like he was volunteering for something. "I could help you with getting things turned around."

"I'm fine," Janie said, not knowing what he was offering but instinctively not trusting it. "I don't need any help."

He raised one eyebrow. "Good luck, then. It's just that if you ask around, you'll find your neighbors are thinking a little different."

# Chapter 3

# MILAN

# JUST GONE

MILAN HAD NEVER SEEN MS. ROBBINS'S CAR BEFORE. IT TURNED out to be a red Mazda Miata, a sports car that only sat two. Now they zipped through the turns on their way to the town's small airport.

"Are you looking forward to being back in Portland?" Ms. Robbins asked. She downshifted. At least that's what Milan thought had happened. She'd never driven a stick.

"It'll be good to see my friends." Milan pictured Chance's black hair, his eyes so dark they seemed all pupil. Would he be just as upset with her as everyone else was? Or would he understand, at least a little? "But I doubt it'll be for long. My mom's probably having Jenna find a new school."

"Once you're there, I would advise putting your head down and working hard. You're a smart girl."

Milan finished the thought for her. "Even if I don't always act like it." Now that there was clearly no way to fix things, she felt less guarded.

"I didn't say that." Ms. Robbins sighed. "I came to Briar Woods because it tries to help people and the environment. When I was your age, I had a tough time. My parents fought constantly and I started acting out. I ran away more than once. I even got arrested."

"No way! For what?" Milan remembered this from times with her dad, how easy it was to talk in the car.

"I won't go into detail. Let's just say I know what it's like to feel overlooked. Overwhelmed." She sighed. "I wish I could have reasoned with the board, but I'm too new. Even with insurance, the school still has to pay a hefty deductible."

"I'm sorry." Milan meant it but worried it didn't sound like it.

The Miata caught up with an old orange VW Vanagon. Milan squinted at the bumper sticker on the back. NOT ALL WHO WANDER ARE LOST. Hippie wisdom.

"Look, I'm not your headmistress now," Ms. Robbins said, passing the Vanagon. "So this is me, one human being talking to another. I have faith in you, Milan. Once you learn to think before you act, you'll be okay."

The GPS interrupted to say they should turn right in

a quarter mile. After guiding them through a few more turns, it announced their arrival.

"Huh," Ms. Robbins said. "I didn't even know this was here." "This" was an FBO, or fixed base operator, a private terminal for private planes. Milan's mom's plane was already on the tarmac, stairs down. "I'm going to think of this next time I'm in the TSA line."

As they got out, her mom came down the stairs, followed by Jenna.

Her mom's hair was in a French twist. Her foundation was perfect, making her expressionless face look even more masklike. She walked over, right hand outstretched. Milan could see the tension in the set of her shoulders.

"Ms. Robbins."

"Senator Mayhew. I appreciate you coming right away."

Her mother looked all angles and edges. Like if Milan tried to hug her, she would cut herself. After her dad died, her mom had lost all interest in eating, forgotten her love of cooking. Now she looked even thinner than when Milan had last seen her, seven weeks ago.

Her mom's eyes narrowed as she took in Milan's blue hair and black roots.

Milan tried to meet her gaze steadily. In some ways, it was like looking in a mirror at her future self. Milan's hair was curlier, but their upturned noses were the same. Her dad's influence was literally in Milan's bones—long legs and long-fingered hands.

She ended their mutual inspection by saying, "Mom, I—"

Her mom raised one finger. "Not now. We can talk about this later."

"I just want to say I'm sorry."

Her mom pressed her lips together so hard they turned into a thin white line. "All I will say, Milan, is that I don't need any more on my plate."

Anger sparked in Milan's veins. Was she just a sprig of parsley her mom could push to the side? Something she would take a single bite of, then spit out in her napkin?

Jenna's face stayed neutral, but Milan saw the smirk in her eyes.

Her mother drew Ms. Robbins to one side and they started talking in low voices.

As the pilot came down the stairs, Milan looked for Eric. But the window of his customary seat was empty.

"Where's Eric?" she asked Jenna. He could always be counted on to be a buffer. If the tension got too thick, he would break it with a weird wager—the next person they saw would be over six feet tall, the next car to pass would be blue, it would rain in the next hour. Eric would bet a dollar on almost anything, and more serious money if it was sports.

Jenna's small nose wrinkled. "This morning, he was putting his suitcase in the overwing when suddenly he just started heaving, right on the tarmac. In front of everyone. It was gross." Her lip curled in disgust. "Eventually he texted us from the bathroom. He said he just was too sick to board."

Milan winced. Nothing was worse than being sick on a plane. Despite all the luxury upgrades, the bathroom on this plane was no bigger than one on a commercial flight. It would be like trying to throw up in an upright coffin.

"He kept telling Heather it was some kind of food poisoning, and since we all ate dinner together last night, none of us should get on the plane. He wasn't making sense. Of course your mother told him that she's got an important meeting in Portland and we couldn't wait. He even called back again, but by that time we were already in the air. He actually tried to talk your mom into getting the plane to land."

The sound of heels made Milan's head turn. Her mom was getting back on the plane. Jenna followed without saying anything else.

Ms. Robbins came over. "I wish you the best, Milan. I truly hope you get your feet under you."

And for a moment, Milan felt understood. Because it was like she had nothing under her. Not her feet, not even the ground. When Ms. Robbins hugged her, she didn't want to let go, but finally she had to. As Ms. Robbins and Milan each took one of her suitcases from the trunk, the pilot came down the stairs. He was a gruff, no-nonsense man. He had flown for them before, but Milan couldn't remember his name. Terry?

"Let's see about your luggage," he said as Ms. Robbins

got back in her car. "It's pretty full inside." The plane had no luggage bins over the seats, only a large compartment in the back. The result was more headroom but less space for suitcases.

Milan followed him to one of the wing lockers, then waved as Ms. Robbins pulled out of the lot. When the pilot opened the locker, inside was Eric's left-behind suitcase, its scuffed silver exterior testifying to the thousands of miles he had flown. The pilot squeezed in one of her suitcases, then swung the door closed and latched it. Taking the other suitcase, he walked around to the second wing locker.

Milan took a deep breath and boarded. The interior was understated: gray carpet, silver quilted leather chairs, white curved walls. The main part of the cabin was taken up by four spacious seats facing each other in pairs. In between, large black folding tables were covered with cell phones, laptops, and paperwork. Her mom and Jenna were in two of the seats, and Mark Smithee, her mom's legislative director, occupied a third. He nodded at Milan as she walked past and took the seat directly behind her mom, one of two behind the main grouping.

Milan unzipped her coat but didn't take it off. She put in her earbuds and closed her eyes, trying to lose herself in her music. In only a few minutes, they were in the air.

The engines droned steadily. More than just a sound, it was a bone-deep vibration, nearly lulling her to sleep. Milan resisted the temptation. If her mom saw, she would think Milan wasn't taking this whole thing seriously. She didn't need to make her mom any madder than she already was. Instead Milan took out her phone.

**Hey,** she texted Chance. **On my way home.** She hadn't texted him since the fire and hadn't answered his two texts. It was unlike them to go so long without being in touch, but she had felt ashamed.

He answered right away. **For good?**

**I wish. Prob just the weekend. Then off to parts unknown.**

**Did u get kicked out again?**

**Guilty as charged.**

**SMH.** She could picture it, Chance shaking his head, one side of his generous mouth curling up even as he tried to frown.

**It was only a little fire.**

**R u joking?**

**Sadly, no.**

Three dots that meant he was typing appeared, then disappeared, then appeared again. Chance must be struggling to find the right thing to say.

As if there was one.

While she waited, Milan peered down at the mountain stretched out below them. The peak poked above cotton-ball puffs of clouds. All white snow and black rocks, it looked like an island in an ocean. Only instead of water it was bordered on all sides by the green of the forest.

A sudden enormous bang made her jump. Her mouth

fell open as she struggled to process what she was seeing. A cloud of dense black smoke billowed just outside the window. When it thinned, she saw most of the wing was just . . . gone. Gone! From behind the cockpit's curtain came a cacophony of alarms as the pilot fought to control the damaged plane.

"Pull up! Pull up!" a mechanical voice warned. The mountain that had been below them was now at a crazy angle.

"Brace!" her mom screamed. "Brace, Milan!"

Milan pressed her face against her knees and laced her hands over the back of her neck. Already knowing it would not be enough.

# Chapter 4

## LENNY
# SLIP INTO THE DARKNESS

LENNY CHECKED THE FLIGHTAWARE APP.

Earlier, it had displayed a lengthening green line pulled along by a tiny green plane. Senator Mayhew's plane. A few seconds ago, Lenny had dialed a number. The call had triggered an old cell phone wired to a bomb inside a suitcase on Senator Mayhew's plane. The second senator Mayhew. Now the second *late* senator Mayhew. Because now the green line was just . . . gone.

It was easy for Lenny to imagine the bomb's aftermath. The air heavy with the smells of broken evergreens and jet fuel. Twisted metal and twisted bodies scattered over the side of the mountain. White snow. Black rocks. Red blood. Likely red flames as well. The plane's wheels were made of magnesium, and if they caught, the conflagration would create its own oxygen as it burned, making extinguishing it nearly impossible.

Normally, search and rescue would be activated once a plane was two hours overdue. But the pilot had been flying by VFR, visual flight rules, which meant no filed flight plan. Without a flight plan for the senator's private plane, there would be no "overdue." And while the plane did have an emergency locator beacon, it was an older type that wasn't always reliable. It also required another airplane to be nearby to hear it.

How long would it be before anyone even realized the senator's plane was missing?

Now Lenny selected a name in the contacts list and pressed it. It was answered after just one ring.

"It's me." She paused. "It's done."

"You're sure?" the client asked.

"I'll be sending up the drone, but I just watched it disappear from the radar."

And with the downed plane went any secrets the people on board had carried. All the loose ends tied off with the press of a button.

The client grunted. "Good."

Lenny slipped the phone back into her pocket.

# Chapter 5

## MILAN

# BEFORE SHE EVEN HAD A CHANCE

MILAN PRESSED HER FACE INTO HER LAP. THE DENIM OF HER JEANS was soft against her cheeks. Her eyes were squeezed closed so tightly they hurt. Was this even real?

Time stalled and then stood still.

Maybe she had fallen asleep in Ms. Robbins's car on the way to the airport, and now she was having a nightmare. Milan tried to will herself awake, to find a different reality, but it didn't work.

She wasn't dreaming. This *was* reality.

Milan wormed her hand between her thighs and belly. After she found the cloth tongue of the seat belt protruding from the cold metal buckle, she pulled it tighter, then pinched her phone and wiggled it free. Head still against her knees, she slid the phone into her back pocket. Then she layered her hands on her neck, tightening them over the knots of bone that seemed scant protection for her spinal cord.

The plane tipped right and left, rocked up and down. It felt like the world's worst roller coaster.

Jenna was screaming. Mark was yelling that everyone should stay calm. The plane itself was squealing and groaning like an injured animal. Punctuating those sounds were the alarms beeping and squawking in the cockpit. As he struggled to straighten out the plane, the pilot was shouting curses. Only Milan's mom, like Milan, was quiet.

Even with her eyes closed, Milan's body felt that the plane was no longer flying in a straight line. The remaining engine roared, increasing thrust in an effort to maintain their airspeed. But without the missing engine to counterbalance it, the plane was beginning to bank left, away from the one working engine. And because it was no longer balanced by matching wings, the plane began to rotate. Milan slid into the wall, which was trying hard to turn itself into the floor.

It was how she had felt with Ms. Robbins. Empty space and her falling through it.

Only a few seconds had passed.

As the nose dipped even farther, a giant hand pushed Milan back. Her stomach crammed into her throat. The change in pressure threatened to burst her eardrums. Still doubled over, she clawed out her earbuds as she opened her eyes. The white earbuds slid away on the gray carpet, disappearing under her mother's seat.

She straightened up. What was the point of bracing? Nothing could protect her from what was about to happen. Outside the window, past the splintered stub of the wing, the evergreens and the snow were much closer. It felt like they were standing still and it was actually the ground heaving itself up to meet them.

Yellow oxygen masks fell from overhead, dangling from clear plastic tubes. Totally forgetting about the rule to put on your own mask first, her mother screamed, "Milan! Put on your mask!"

Milan slipped the white elastic strap over her head and pressed the yellow cone over her mouth and nose. The scent of new plastic filled her nostrils. The limp plastic bag dangling from the front of the mask seemed no more substantial than a sandwich bag.

In her muscles and sinews, she could feel that while they were still angling toward the ground, the descent was no longer as steep. The plane seemed to be straightening out, too, because the floor was once again the floor.

Larry or Jerry—hadn't he told her once he'd flown planes in Iraq or Afghanistan or something? Maybe he could gently bring them down. Maybe he could find a patch of pillowy snow and they would skim along the surface, gradually coming to a halt. Exclaiming at their luck, they would clamber out and wait for rescue.

23

Then the plane jerked to the left, slamming Milan against the curved white plastic wall. Now even Mark was screaming. The plane was in a monster's jaws, being shaken back and forth.

Before the car accident that had broken her leg and killed her dad, death had seemed impossible to Milan. Something that might happen to other people, but never to her. The crash had ripped away her secret belief that no matter what happened, *she* was always going to be safe.

She had barely escaped death once. Now it was returning to finish the job. Milan was going to die before she even had a chance to live.

Her mom's hand reached back, blindly groping. Milan grabbed her fingers and squeezed.

In the cockpit, a computerized voice spoke over the warning pings and squawks. "Low terrain. Low terrain," it announced in an oddly cheerful tone.

They needed more altitude, more space, more time.

They weren't going to get any of those things.

The evergreens were even closer now, so close Milan could no longer see the snow. Maybe the trees could cushion their fall, catching the plane in their limbs.

Treetops began to brush the underside of the plane. Then the cabin filled with a gritty screech as trunks scraped under their feet. First the floor vibrated and then the whole plane shook. Dark evergreens flickered past the windows like an accelerated movie reel.

The noise was thunderous. With a scream of tearing metal, the remaining wing disappeared. A shower of electrical sparks rained down orange bits of light.

They weren't flying anymore, Milan admitted to herself.

They weren't gliding.

Across the aisle, Jenna pressed her hands to the sides of her face. Her eyes were wide, mouth hanging open in a scream.

They were falling.

The pilot was doing his best, but Milan would never get a chance to figure out his name.

She would never get a chance to figure out anything.

The roar was now so loud it engulfed all her other senses, including her sense of self.

"Milan!"

"Mom!" Milan screamed back inside her mask, squeezing her mom's hand tighter. "Mom!"

They met the ground.

And time disintegrated.

# Chapter 6

JANIE

# NEVER SAY NEVER

**Three years earlier**

JANIE AND THE MAN, WHOSE NAME WAS STEVE, SAT AT HER OLD oak kitchen table, cups of coffee steaming in front of them. Becca was at the restaurant where she worked a few times a week, the kids were at school, and Thad was in town running errands. Janie had had to put Rocky in the laundry room. For a guy who'd never been a dairy farmer, Steve was surprisingly well versed in bedding, baleage, and rotation grazing.

Guessing he might not have heard the joke, Janie said, "You know what they say. Dairy farming is a lot like prison, except in prison you don't have to get up twice a day and milk the guards."

Steve threw his head back in a laugh. His teeth were white and even, making Janie think about how Noelle needed braces. Then he got serious. "You ever think about getting one of those robotic systems that milk the cows for you?"

Now it was Janie's turn to laugh, but there was no humor in it. "They cost like a couple hundred thousand."

Steve acted like a smart guy, but he was a fool if he thought she had that kind of money. Buying one of those systems was about as likely as hiring space aliens to work the land. With them, the cows were milked whenever they felt like it, twenty-four hours a day. After a cow walked into a milking stall, the robot's mechanical arms sanitized each teat before attaching laser-guided suction cups. Meanwhile, the cow got a snack as incentive.

"Never say never," Steve said. "Because the deals your neighbors are making with Prospect Power mean they're already talking about planting orchards, buying new tractors, and putting money back into their land." He smiled again. "So there might just be a robot milker in your future."

# Chapter 7

## MILAN

# A MESS OF BLOOD AND BONE

SHE WOKE IN DARKNESS, HER MOUTH TASTING LIKE METAL. WHERE was she? Who was she? How was she? But it was like reaching into a black, empty space. Her mind couldn't grab on to anything.

Nearby, someone was moaning softly.

She held her breath to hear better. The moans stopped. She let herself breathe again, and the sounds started up.

The moans were coming from her.

Suddenly, everything came back. Ms. Robbins taking her to the airport. The explosion. Putting on her mask. The plane spiraling downward. Holding her mom's hand as everyone screamed. The ground rushing up. The darkness. Milan remembered all of it now.

She raised her head, wincing at a twinge in her neck. Her questions took on even greater urgency. How badly was she hurt? What about her mom? The sounds from when they were still airborne had ceased: the screams and the alarms, the deep groans of the plane being torn apart. All she could hear now was something dripping and a faint whistling noise.

The plane had landed on its left side, the nose lower than the tail. Now Milan lay on her left side against what had been the wall of the plane, still curled in a sitting position even though her seat had turned ninety degrees. Her oxygen mask now rested near her right ear. She pulled it off.

The air was icy. She breathed in the sharp scent of fresh-cut pine, like Christmas trees. But layered over that was another smell. Oily. Acrid. It must be jet fuel.

Find her mom. That was the most important thing.

Milan turned her head to the right, ignoring the pinch in her neck. A ten-foot-long hole had been torn along the other side of the plane, which was now the ceiling. The whistling sound was the wind.

"Mom!" she yelled into the near silence. "Anybody?"

In answer, a groan rose and hung in the air. Milan didn't know whose it was, just that it wasn't hers. She wasn't alone, then.

"I'm coming." With shaking hands, she fumbled with the seat belt until it opened. Her left ring finger was bent at an odd angle, but she had more important things to worry about.

Getting to her knees, she grabbed the side of her mom's seat for balance. For one horrifying moment, she took in the rest of the cabin. Then she let the edges of her vision blur, refusing to think about anything but her mom. She was Milan's only priority.

When she peered over the seat, her mom was doubled over the folding table, lying on the wall turned floor.

"Mom?" Ignoring the others, ignoring the pain when she steadied her left hand on the seat, Milan leaned over and shook her mom's shoulder. Her mom's face turned, but was it just because Milan had moved her? The oxygen mask was still over her face, so Milan couldn't see if she was breathing. Fear and hope fought each other as she moved her hand to her mom's neck, just above her pale blue cashmere sweater. Warm. Was her mom alive and unconscious? Dead but still warm?

"Mom?" Milan repeated, her voice shaking. Every part of her was shaking, from cold and fear and the effort it was taking not to think about certain things. Her breath was a little cloud in front of her face. Grabbing her mom's wrist, she searched for a pulse. Under her fingertips, a faint flutter, so soft it took a moment to be sure. At least her mom was alive.

Her mom moaned. But she didn't move.

Trying to speak in a soothing tone, Milan said, "Okay, Mom, hold on, we're going to get you out."

Where had that *we* come from? Because right now it

was just her, and she had no idea what to do. But she had to do something. Before this plane became their metal tomb.

Only now did Milan let herself look at Jenna and Mark for longer than a split second. Mark had been seated in the same row as her mom, on the other side of the aisle, next to the side of the plane that had been ripped away. His long legs dangled across the aisle. The foot closest to Milan was turned the wrong way.

When she allowed herself to focus on Mark's face, a cold fist of horror squeezed her heart. He was clearly dead. Above the bright yellow snout of his mask, his blue eyes were open, but the right side of his skull was sunken, his graying hair matted with blood.

Across from him, Jenna startled with a gasp. She groaned and pushed her hair off her face, which was covered in bright red blood. Her hands fumbled with her seat belt, the only thing keeping her in her seat. If she succeeded in freeing herself, she would fall from one side of the plane to the other.

"Hold on, Jenna, just hold on for a second," Milan yelled.

Was help on the way? How long would it take? How was Milan going to treat their injuries? How was she going to keep them warm? Did she need to get them out? With the plane on its side, the door was also pressed against the snow.

The pilot. He would know what to do. Trying not to

touch anything with her broken finger, Milan squeezed past her mom and clambered over the empty seat that would have held Eric. Her Doc Martens slid on the thin layer of snow dusting the plastic wall turned floor. When she reached the door that could be flipped down to make stairs, she balanced on the edges of two while pulling open the stiff charcoal curtain.

On the other side sat the pilot, or what had been the pilot. A tree trunk had speared first through the windshield and then through him. Above his uniform was just a mess of blood and bone.

# Chapter 8

## MILAN

# A MONSTER, BREATHING

LOOKING AT THE DEAD PILOT, MILAN WANTED TO SLUMP DOWN and cry. She wanted to wake up in Ms. Robbins's car. She wanted an adult to take over. She wanted her mom.

Only a few seconds had passed since she had regained consciousness, but each one felt like it had lasted hours.

Where even were they? Someplace in the Cascade Mountains, she guessed. The nearest inhabited place was probably dozens of miles away. And even if it was closer, help wasn't going to arrive immediately. Everyone else was dead or injured. It was all up to her.

*Think*, Milan commanded herself. *Be smart. Think! What would Dad do?*

As she turned back, she nearly lost her balance, catching herself with her left hand. A scream forced itself from her throat. Her already swollen finger now throbbed with every beat of her heart. She turned back. The tail of the plane had cracked, and daylight was leaking in.

But she only had eyes for her mom. Her head was up, which was good. She had even managed to get her mask off. But she wasn't returning Milan's gaze. She wasn't focused on anything.

As Milan got closer, her breath stilled in her chest. A dark trickle of blood was running from her mom's right ear. Was her mom broken inside?

Jenna was moaning again. And layered over it was a new sound, only a bit louder than the wind.

It sounded like a monster, breathing.

*Fire*, Milan's brain whispered. *Fire*.

Her mom lifted her hand and pointed behind Milan.

Milan looked back. A delicate orange flame edged up one side of the cockpit curtain, fragile as a dream. Then it curled over like a cresting wave and raced down. A spark fell on the carpet and the flames danced toward them. The air smelled of burning plastic, rubber, and jet fuel.

As Milan scrambled back toward her mom, cold dotted her cheeks. Snowflakes were lightly falling through the torn side of the plane.

*The only way out is through*. Another thing her dad used to say. Milan touched her tattoo. In this case, the only way out was through the side of the plane, past sharp-edged metal. But at least there was a way out.

Crouching, she clawed at her mom's seat belt. Her eyes burned from the heat and smoke. The fire was only about six feet away from Milan's back, and three from Jenna's. It was going to eat them up.

The belt refused to open, no matter how much she pried on the buckle. But there was some slack across her mom's hips. "Push back and slide your legs out," Milan urged.

"Milan," Jenna moaned from across the aisle. "Help me. Help me get out." Blood was dripping from her hair.

"Just a sec. Let me get my mom first."

Milan wouldn't think about how the fire was closer to Jenna than to her mom. Her mom had to come first.

With Milan's assistance, her mom slipped free. But when Milan took her hands away, her mom slumped against the wall as if all her energy had been exhausted.

Pulling off her coat, Milan used it to pad the worst of the sharp edges where the side of the plane was peeled back like the lid of a tin can.

Heat was beginning to scald the back of her legs. Milan looped her arms under her mom's shoulders so she was both hugging her and supporting her. How long had it been since they were this close? With her nose buried in her mother's hair, the familiar scent of Chanel No. 5 momentarily displaced the reek of burning plastic and jet fuel.

With her right foot Milan stepped back and up, onto the armrest, the one belonging to Mark's seat. She managed to get her left foot on the armrest, too. With a grunt, she straightened her legs, taking her mom's full weight. Now both their heads were in the cold, fresh air. Milan gulped it eagerly, gathering strength.

Somehow she managed to hoist her mom half through the opening. Milan got her hands underneath her butt and pushed. The move wrenched her broken finger. She shrieked, tears springing to her eyes. It didn't matter, though, it didn't matter—she just had to get her mom out. Terror gave her strength. Then her mom's hips were up and over the edge. Milan grabbed her mom's bare feet and used them to push her farther out of the plane.

Suddenly gravity took over, and her mom disappeared as she slid along the curved body of the plane and presumably plopped onto the snowy ground.

Milan turned back to look for Jenna. The smoke was so heavy that at first she didn't see her. And then she wished she hadn't.

The fire was leaping on Jenna now, hungry. Devouring. Jenna was twisting, screaming wordlessly, eaten by flames.

Milan couldn't save her now. She probably couldn't even save herself. Her feet scrambled, trying to find purchase to get herself higher. She stepped on something that might have been Mark's head, but she told herself Mark was dead. She couldn't hurt him. With a leap, Milan belly flopped onto the outside of the plane, her lower legs still inside.

The fire was right beneath her, roaring and twisting and clawing at her calves. Milan managed to lift her legs and pivot so they rested on the outside of the plane.

Jenna's shrieks took on a new pitch and then stopped altogether. Milan closed her eyes. She couldn't have saved Jenna. If she had tried, she would have had to abandon her mother. But Jenna's plea still echoed in her mind. What if she had taken just a second? Could she have saved her?

But then she felt her eyebrows singeing. The smell of charred flesh and burning hair broke through her shock. The heat of the flames physically pushed her back. Milan grabbed her coat, already peppered with melted spots, and let herself slide bonelessly to the ground.

# Chapter 9

## MILAN
# ON THE COUNT OF THREE

MILAN LANDED IN THE SNOW. A FEW FEET AWAY, HER MOM LAY sprawled on her side, eyes closed. Her breathing was fast and shallow, but the fact that she was breathing at all seemed a miracle. Why hadn't Milan tried to grab her before she slid to the ground? Had she got hurt even worse?

Her back against the plane, Milan put her hands over her face. It was all too much. The explosion, the crash, the fire. The three people who had just died. And now, if anything was going to be done, it was all up to her.

*Woman up*, Milan ordered herself, trying to channel Ms. Robbins. She dropped her hands and crawled toward her mom.

Her mom's French twist had come loose, and her dark

hair was fanned around her head. Her bare legs were only partly covered by her dark wool skirt, but at least the rest of her was dressed in layers—pale blue cashmere sweater, navy blue suit jacket, and a long double-breasted camel-colored cashmere coat. The coat was unbuttoned, rucked up behind her. If her mom's injuries didn't kill her, the cold soon might. Her luggage was burning along with everything— and everyone, Milan's brain reminded her—else.

The plane radiated heat. The snow on the ground was turning slushy, and more was falling from the sky. Could the moisture douse the flames? Her hopeful thought died before it was completed. Just like you couldn't put out a gasoline fire with water, snow wouldn't stop this blaze. It would burn until the fuel was gone. Since Gary or Harry didn't seem to have refueled when they picked her up, with luck there wasn't much fuel left.

But even if the fire didn't eat through the plane, hypo-thermia would just kill them a different way.

"Mom?" Milan leaned closer. Her mom's lips appeared violet, nearly blue. Maybe it was just a trick of the light reflecting off the snow. "Mom?" she repeated. Her heart pulsed in her ears, the hollow of her throat, her broken finger.

Her mother's eyelids fluttered and finally opened.

"Do you think you can move?" Milan asked. "We need to get away from the plane. It's on fire."

Her mom didn't answer. After blinking a couple of

times, she closed her eyes. She didn't seem capable of walking or even crawling.

So Milan was going to have to move her.

Maybe she could drag her. Milan got to her feet and gripped her mom's shoulders. But if she dragged her like that, her mom's head and neck would be unsupported.

Letting go of her mom's coat, Milan reached for her Columbia coat, the one she had used to pad the torn edges of the plane. She spread it out next to her mom. Trying to keep her mother's spine aligned, with one hand on her shoulder and the other on her hip, Milan gently turned her on her side, then steadied her with her left palm. With her other hand, Milan pulled the cashmere coat down and then slid her own coat under her mom's head and upper body. Gently, she rolled her back.

As Milan got to her feet, the plane groaned. A huge plume of fire bloomed out of the torn side.

She grabbed the top corners of her coat and lifted them so they cradled her mom's head. "Okay, on the count of three, I'm going to move you."

Her mom's eyes opened. Her mouth opened, too, but instead of saying anything she just licked her lips and nodded.

"One," Milan said. "Two." She straightened her legs. "Three." She shuffled backward, ignoring how her back protested. Her mom made a sound between a scream and a moan, and after a split-second pause, Milan ignored that, too. A cold gust of air chilled the sweat on her face.

Flames unfurled down the side of the plane. Milan crab-walked backward even faster.

Her eyes went from the flames to her mom's face and back again. Despite how much she was trying not to jostle her, a fresh trickle of bright blood ran past her mom's gold hoop earring and down the side of her neck.

Finally Milan felt like they were far enough away to be safe. All they had to do was survive until help came. To do that, they needed to be warmer. Her teeth were chattering even when she tried to hold them apart. She could take her coat back from her mom, but her mom needed it more.

Unlike her mom, Milan still had shoes: her Doc Martens. But while her mom was dressed in wool, Milan was wearing jeans. *Cotton kills*—she remembered that from her dad. Wet, it didn't hold warmth. And—she patted her butt with her good hand—her seat was definitely damp from sitting in half-melted snow. Her phone was still in her pocket. When she pulled it out, it read "No service." It was 10:12 AM. Seven or so hours until the sun set.

She turned in a circle. Other than the wreckage, there were no signs of civilization, not even a contrail in the sky. Ahead of them, the mountain. Black cliffs sliced through the peak of white snow like obsidian knives. Milan suddenly felt small. Insignificant. She and her mom were two dark specks on an immense white canvas. Like ants, waiting to be stepped on.

The plane's belly had left a divot in the snow. They had ended up just above the tree line: tall triangles of evergreens, branches heavy with snow. There would be no dry ground underneath to offer them shelter.

Bits of twisted metal lay everywhere. The second wing, the one that hadn't exploded, was lodged high in the branches of a tree about three hundred feet away.

Milan hugged her arms to her chest, the left one on top to avoid putting any pressure on her broken finger, attempting to still her trembling. It was lightly snowing. They needed more layers if they were going to survive until help came. In that wing locker was one of her suitcases. Maybe someone else's, too.

All she had to do was get them.

# Chapter 10

## MILAN

# THEY'LL COME AFTER YOU

MILAN SQUATTED NEXT TO HER MOM. HER EYES WERE CLOSED. WAS she even conscious?

"Mom, I'll be right back. I think I can get us some warmer clothes."

Her mom spoke. Or rather, whispered. "Hurts."

Heedless of the snow, Milan fell to her knees. "Where?"

Her mom's eyes opened and her pale lips turned up in something that wasn't really a smile. "Everywhere."

She grabbed her mom's cold hand. "Help has to be coming." The only pressure in their grip was coming from Milan. It was still a comfort.

"No flight plan." Her mom shook her head, then stopped

with a wince. "You have to leave." Her sentences were chunks of three or four words.

"Leave? Why?"

"They'll come after you."

Milan's brows drew together. Exactly how hard had her mom hit her head? "Who will?"

"Whoever killed Jack." Her mom's voice strengthened. "And blew up the plane."

"Dad died in a car accident." Milan gave voice to the hardest truth, the one she tried to hide even from herself. "We were arguing and I distracted him." The worst part was that it had been about something inconsequential, both of them too stubborn to admit they were wrong.

"Oh, Milan." Her mom's other hand rose to touch Milan's cheek and then fell back on her chest. "Your dad . . . found something. So they killed him."

"What?" Milan felt dizzy. She'd been there. Her dad hadn't been shot or poisoned or stabbed. Instead, while he and Milan had been arguing, he had drifted out of his lane and into the path of the car behind them. The resulting crash had caused the RAV4 Hybrid to flip.

As for the plane, it had to have been a bird strike. Her dad had always worried about those.

Her mom must have been confused from hitting her head and the beginnings of hypothermia. Milan couldn't do anything about her injuries, but she could get both of them warmer.

"The first thing we need to do is get you warm. You're literally freezing to death. We both are." After giving her mom's hand one last squeeze, Milan stood up. "I think I can get us some more clothes. I'll be back as soon as I can."

# Chapter 11

## JANIE
# AFFORD TO IGNORE

**Three years earlier**

STEVE SET DOWN HIS COFFEE CUP AND SIGHED. "RIGHT NOW, PROS-pect is in a generous mood." He lifted one shoulder. "And once they have a big enough stake, well, who knows, but they might not be so generous. When the exploration starts in earnest, they can choose who has the most promising property and who they can afford to ignore."

Could Janie afford to ignore Steve? Every night she lay awake in the queen bed that still, after all these years, felt far too big. Tossing and turning until the sheets wound around her, she would fret about robbing Peter to pay Paul. Trying to figure out what could wait and what could be bought on credit, when it all needed to be done now.

Could this be the miracle she had been praying for?

# Chapter 12

# LENNY
# STILL ALIVE

### Ten months ago

LENNY HAD PULLED A STOLEN HONDA NEARLY ALONGSIDE JACK Mayhew's Toyota RAV4 Hybrid, aligned the Honda's front wheels with the rear wheels of his SUV. The phone on her dash was filming the whole thing. After an initial gentle sideways bump, she had sped up while simultaneously steering sharply into the back end of the RAV4. As Jack's car skidded, turning in front of her, Lenny accelerated while moving out of the lane, eyes on the rearview mirror. It all went according to plan. The mismatched bumpers and the RAV4's higher center of gravity caused it to roll over several times. It landed on the driver's side.

After pulling over, Lenny had grabbed the phone with one gloved hand and run back to the car. They'd been the only two on the road, but that wouldn't last long. The windshield had turned into a blanket of cracked glass. The air was still hazy from the powder that had coated the air-bags, now deflated white balloons. Jack was suspended by his seat belt, head limp, body as loose as a rag doll's. Lenny braced one hand on the roof turned wall, leaned in over the kid's body, and checked Jack's throat for a pulse. Nothing. After pulling Jack's wallet from his back pocket, she strained for his bag on the back seat.

And then jumped at the sound of a moan. Coming from the passenger seat. Lenny looked down.

The girl was still alive. Milan. Her left leg was wedged in the crumpled footwell, twisted at an impossible angle, a lump under her bloody jeans where it should be smooth. Blood was starting to puddle on the passenger-side door. Blood always looked like more than it was, but this was still a lot.

The daughter hadn't been the target, but the client had given the green light to kill anyone in Jack's general vicinity. After all, it wasn't their fault the senator was hardly ever alone.

Suddenly Lenny's fingers went to Jack's belt buckle, tugged the belt free, and with some contortions managed to lean in and squeeze it under Milan's thigh. The girl made a protesting sound, even though her eyes didn't open. Lenny pulled the belt tight.

And then quickly walked away. Two other cars had

pulled over. People were just getting out of their cars, eyes and mouths wide with shock.

"I've called the police," Lenny had lied, waving the burner phone that had filmed all the important bits. "They're on their way."

# Chapter 13

MILAN

# ONE STEP AT A TIME

"I'LL BE RIGHT BACK, MOM," MILAN SAID. SHE WAS AFRAID TO leave, but she didn't have a choice.

Her mom's expression didn't change. Her eyes were at half-mast. Her bare feet looked like they had been cleverly fashioned out of wax, ivory against the blinding white of the snow. The snow drifting down was filling up the rut Milan had made dragging her mom away from the plane.

Boots scuffing, Milan ran the three hundred feet to the tree where the airplane wing had lodged. The air smelled sharply of evergreens. The wing was about twenty feet up, balanced precariously on broken branches. Standing underneath and trying to shake it loose would not be smart.

She grabbed one of the lower branches on the other side of the tree and yanked it down. A lightning bolt ran from her broken finger all the way up her arm, and a clump of snow plopped on her head. She gasped as an icy fistful slid down her neck and finally stopped at the waistband of her jeans.

As she shook snow from her hair, Milan used her right hand to scoop out snow from the back of her jeans. She looked at her left hand. The skin around her first knuckle was turning green and purple, the creases puffed out to flat dark lines.

She needed both hands. She needed a doctor with an X-ray machine and a padded metal splint. At a minimum, she needed some medical tape so she could buddy tape the broken finger to the one next to it.

But then she remembered what her mom used to say when there didn't seem to be anything in the house for dinner. *You have to work with what you have.* And somehow they would sit down to an amazing meal her mom had pulled together of odds and ends from the pantry and fridge.

Milan steadied herself on a branch, stood on one foot, and pulled off her other boot. She tugged off the sock and then pulled the boot back over her bare foot. How long until she had frostbite?

But even if she lost toes or fingers, it didn't matter. All that mattered was living. Today she had seen death, heard death, even smelled it. She pushed the thoughts away.

She wrapped the sock twice around her ring and middle fingers, then pulled the mouth snugly over her whole hand, like a mitten. She flexed her fingers experimentally. They moved more or less as a unit.

Once again, she grabbed the branch and whipped it up and down, imagining it was a battle rope in gym.

A loud creak came from the top of the tree. Milan looked up. The wing slid an inch, two. Then it stopped. When she tried again, it didn't even budge.

Okay. Time for plan B. Climb the tree until she got close enough to the wing to shove it loose.

She pushed toward the trunk, sinking into snow that, sheltered by the overhanging branches, got looser with every step. Once she reached the trunk, she studied it for a possible route. The branches more or less alternated with each other on either side. The trick would be getting started.

"Okay," she said out loud. "One step at a time." Another thing her dad used to say.

Milan curled her hands around a chin-high branch. With a hard exhale, she jumped up, planning to straighten her elbows. In her head, she saw herself locking them out, like a gymnast mounting a balance beam, and then swinging a leg over.

Her jump wasn't nearly high enough. She tried again, trying to explode upward, but the snow was too soft to push off of, and she still ended up a good six inches short. She was never going to be able to do this.

Then Milan thought of her mom, injured, unmoving, her feet already the color of bone. She could not let her only remaining parent die because she was afraid. Because she was weak.

This time she focused on getting one leg over the branch. On her second try, she managed to catch the top of it with the edge of her right knee. Twisting, she hooked her leg over so she was balanced on her belly on top of the branch, then crawled to the trunk.

Clinging to the trunk like a koala, she pulled herself to her feet, ignoring how the bark bit through her clothes. At least the trunk was warmer than the ambient air, which she guessed was in the high twenties.

Grabbing a higher branch, she stepped her right foot up to the next branch, then repeated the move on her left side. Feeling like Spider-Man, Milan made a point of not looking down. One branch at a time, she inched upward. Two hours ago, she would have said what she was doing was impossible. But now even the impossible still had to be accomplished. If she didn't do this, her mom would freeze to death.

Right hand. Right foot. Left hand. Left foot.

The higher she climbed, the farther she could see. All around her, nothing but trees and snow. No signs of civilization. They could be anywhere. They could be nowhere.

Wait. What was that? Far ahead, a dark thread cut through the snow. A stream? Her dad always said if you got lost hiking, you should stay put. But he'd also said that if you followed water downhill, you would eventually find civilization. All water was connected, from the water of a forest stream to the water that ran from their taps.

When she was still several feet from the wing, Milan heard a faint whine. Clinging even more tightly to the trunk, she turned her head. Through a gap in the snowy branches, she could see her mom, lying where Milan had left her.

But now, hovering over her still form was a small gray object not much bigger than a shoebox. The corners of it were a blur. Propellors.

It was a drone, hovering a few feet above her mother's face. As if whoever was piloting the drone was inspecting her.

Help was coming! The rescuers must be pinpointing their location.

Milan's mouth made a smacking noise as she opened it to shout. Then her mom's words echoed in her head.

*They'll come after you. . . . Whoever killed Jack. And blew up the plane.*

# Chapter 14

## LENNY
# DISPOSABLE

THUMBS ON THE JOYSTICKS, EYES ON THE IPAD CONNECTED TO THE controller, Lenny stood on the old logging road and piloted the drone the seven miles to the crash site. All those years spent playing video games with Karl made the moves almost second nature.

Lenny had always called him Karl. Never Dad. Just like Karl had called her Lenny, never Lena.

A few days ago, Lenny had bought an old Subaru for cash, lied that she would file the paperwork to register it, and then driven it to Bend. The drive of eleven hours and change was worth not having to put bags through an airport X-ray machine. Not when the contents of those bags—the drone, several wigs, assorted weapons—might raise questions.

People came to Bend to hike and kayak, to swim in the summer and ski in the winter. They came for the more than a dozen award-winning independent breweries.

They usually didn't come with the aim of bringing down a senator's plane.

By law, you couldn't fly a drone higher than four hundred feet or out of your line of sight. Of course, violating FAA regulations paled in comparison with breaking the laws against assassination and murder. Good thing Lenny didn't care about any of them.

The FAA rules also said you couldn't fly near planes or over people, but the senator's plane would now be a heap of burning metal and plastic, and all the people on board would be dead. You also couldn't fly a drone near an emergency, so as not to interfere with first responders. By the time anyone arrived at the scene of this crash, though, their only task would be retrieving the remains.

The iPad's screen was filled with a bird's-eye view of tall, snow-covered triangles of evergreens interspersed with a few leafless deciduous trees. Lenny adjusted the angle of the camera attached to the drone. The top third of the screen, where the trees ended and the mountain continued, was even more stark—white snow, black rock outcroppings, white sky.

There.

Lenny felt a jolt of adrenaline. Just past the tree line was a small smear of black on the expanse of white. As if someone had tried to erase a charcoal drawing, leaving behind a feathery black smudge.

The drone tracked to the left, neatly avoiding an especially tall tree. It had automatic omnidirectional object avoidance and had cost more than a used car. Karl would have loved it.

The wreckage became clearer. Just as Lenny had expected, the plane had caught fire. Flickers of red danced around the blackened fuselage. White smoke rose as white snow fell. On the screen, the snowflakes shimmered like static.

Lenny had paid someone to slip the bomb into Eric's luggage. It hadn't looked like a bomb, of course. It had been disguised as a present.

The bomb had reduced one wing to a stub. The other had been sheared off by a tree and was now caught in its branches. Unidentifiable bits and pieces were scattered over the snow.

What was unexpected was the figure stretched out on the ground a hundred feet from the plane. A woman, Lenny thought, but more than that was hard to see from this distance through the falling snow. Was it Heather Mayhew, the senator? Her assistant, Jenna Spencer? Or the senator's daughter, Milan?

She flew closer, then flipped a switch to hover the drone, reducing motion blur, thumbs ready to correct any anomalies. A fire could do crazy things to the air, creating its own eddies and turbulence.

Peering at the screen, she moved the sticks to frame the shot. The body was definitely Heather's. The video feed beamed back to the iPad was grainy, similar to a baby monitor. The SD card on the Hasselblad camera mounted to the gimbal recorded 5.1K video, good enough for a feature film. And that was what Lenny would turn it into, a mini-movie for the client to watch over and over on his wall-sized TV. The proof of his power as much a trophy as a mounted animal head.

A long beat passed. The senator's face was as color-less as the snow dusting down on it like powdered sugar. Lenny squinted, waiting for Heather to move.

She didn't.

Somehow, Heather had lived through the crash. Some-how made her way out. And then finally, Heather had done what she should have in the first place.

Died.

Maybe it was better that she had died in full view like this. Now there was no question as to whether her body was really in the wreckage.

Lenny had been paid to kill first one senator and then his replacement. And now Jack and Heather were both dead. Mission accomplished.

Of course, there was collateral damage. There was always collateral damage. Even the occasional dead girl. Families were generally off-limits, but sometimes it couldn't be helped.

Suddenly, the drone began to gyrate, the images a dizzying blur. It must have been caught by a sudden gust from the smoking wreckage. Now it was a millimeter from flipping completely upside down and boring into the snow.

Quickly working the joysticks, Lenny got the drone righted and then zoomed farther up into the thickening snow. That had been too close. Better to float far above, unaffected. She hit the Return to Home button. The drone would figure out for itself the optimal route back.

It was done now. All the loose ends tied up into a pretty bow. Everyone dead. No one left to ask questions. No one left to betray their friends, for a price. All sacrificed to solve the problem.

Only one thought nagged.

Would the client ever decide Lenny was just as disposable?

# Chapter 15

## MILAN

# ALL TRUE

THE DRONE HOVERING OVER MILAN'S MOTHER'S BODY SUDDENLY began to oscillate. Just when it seemed like it would crash, it straightened out, then rose about a hundred feet into the air. It flew toward the trees. Toward her. As its buzz got louder, Milan tilted her head down and gripped the trunk harder, hoping it couldn't see her.

Just after it flew overhead, her right foot slipped. For what seemed like an eternity, it pedaled in the empty air. Her stomach crammed into the back of her throat. Finally her boot found a small branch. It bent under her weight, threatening to break. Still, it was enough. Milan was able to wrap her legs around the rough trunk, narrower now. Her left hand throbbed, her neck felt pinched, and her breath was coming in gasps. A wave of dizziness made the mossy bark flicker in and out of focus.

A strange creaking made her jerk in panic. She looked up just as the wing narrowly missed her, tumbling to the ground. Her frantic efforts to save herself had jostled it loose.

Milan felt her way back down the tree. About five feet from the ground, she jumped, sinking to her knees in the loose snow.

Her chest felt like someone had unzipped it and stuffed a squirrel inside. Why hadn't her mother moved when the drone hovered over her? Who had been piloting it? What had they seen? And what would they do next?

Milan wanted to close her eyes and curl into a ball so tight she disappeared. She had already seen too much, been asked to do too much.

Instead she hurried to the torn-off wing. Her first priority was finding her mom warm clothes. Then together they could decide what to do.

Each side of the wing locker was secured with a flat silver latch. Milan flipped them up, then lifted the lightweight door. It should have slanted up like a car hood, but the hinges at the top were broken. Shaking again from the cold as well as adrenaline, she let it fall.

In addition to her bag, the locker held Eric's golf clubs and a battered green duffel bag that must have been the pilot's, whatever his name had been. Kerry?

Milan grabbed her suitcase and hurried back to her mom. She wanted to pray, but all she could do was mutter, "Please, please, please," under her breath.

Her mom still lay exactly where Milan had left her. She didn't move at the sound of crunching footsteps. Her eyes were closed. Was she even breathing?

"Mom!" Dropping the bag, Milan crouched next to her. She put her fingers on her wrist. Again the faint flutter, like a moth beating against a window.

Her mother's eyes opened. They were glassy but still managed to focus on her. "Milan?"

"I'm here, Mom." She slipped her fingers down to hold her mom's hand and squeezed. She wouldn't think about how cold it felt, colder even than her own icy hands. Like marble, not flesh. Milan opened her suitcase. It was filled with roll-up compression bags that allowed her to stuff as many clothes as possible into a small space. She pawed through them, looking for the warmest clothes. Looking for some miracle that would save her mother. "We're going to get you warmed up. I've got pants and socks and . . ."

Her mom reached for her hand with limp fingers. "Wait, Milan."

She stilled.

"Was there a drone?" Her mom paused to breathe, but her chest barely moved. "Did I . . . dream that?" Her grasp loosened and slipped away.

"Yeah. It left, though." There! A pair of socks.

"Did it see you?"

"I don't think so." Milan took a deep breath, ignoring how it scoured her lungs. "Before, you were saying something about a bomb." Her words came slower. "And about someone killing Dad."

Her mom nodded.

"But I was with Dad when he died. He lost control of the car because we were arguing about me staying out too late."

Her mom started to shake her head, then winced. "They wanted it to look . . . like an accident."

"How do you know?"

"Jack didn't tell me. Tried to . . . keep me safe." She breathed in between phrases. "Same reason . . . I put you . . . boarding school. I found . . . evidence."

"What did you find?"

Her mom fumbled a ring of keys from her coat pocket. "This."

Milan recognized one of the keys. It had a pink rubber ring around the top so that it stood out from the other keys.

"Dad's keys?" That had been his house key.

Her mom's answer was a whisper with no power behind it. Milan leaned closer. She picked up "proof" and "safe."

In addition to the house key, the key ring held a car fob and four other keys. One was small and made of brass.

*Safe.* Milan thought of the safe in the basement where her parents kept important papers.

"Evidence...inside. Give to Brent."

Brent Kirkby was Milan's godfather. He'd been her dad's mentor from back when Jack was running the renewable power company Mr. Kirkby had started. At the funeral, Mr. Kirkby had literally held up her mom. Afterward, her mom had often turned to him for advice, seeking her own version of WWJD.

"Evidence of what?" Milan asked.

Her mom closed her eyes, the ghost of an annoyed expression moving across her face. "Don't trust...anyone. Only Brent."

"Shouldn't I go to the cops? Or the FBI?"

"No!" Despite the obvious pain it caused, she shook her head. "Eric reached out to them." Her eyes focused on the burning plane, then back on Milan's face. "And this happened." With effort, she spoke more forcefully. "They think...you guys are dead. So you have to...stay dead. You have to...go. Now."

"What? No." Milan shook her head. "I can't leave you."

Her mom's eyes had gone unfocused. "It's too late. Something's...broken inside."

Milan's heart somersaulted. "I'm not leaving you. Besides, we're on the top of a mountain. Where am I going to go?"

"You'll...figure it out." Her mother swallowed and blood spilled over her lips.

"No, Mom. Stay with me. Don't leave me all alone."

"You're never...alone." She turned her hand and touched Milan's wrist, the one with the tattoo to remind her of her dad. "Always...in your heart." There was so little breath behind her words that Milan had to read her lips to be sure of them.

"I don't mean metaphorically." Milan shook her head. The motion made everything spin. "I want you here for real."

"Love you. So much." Blood again breached her lips, the color shocking against her pale skin. "Now go."

"No!" It was hard to breathe.

Her mom's lips moved but no sound at all came out. Her breathing slowed, became raspy. A sharp rattle followed. Her eyes went dull.

"Mom!" Milan grabbed her shoulders and shook, but her body remained limp. She put her ear to her mother's cold lips, tacky with blood.

Her mom wasn't breathing.

No. No. NO.

She wasn't dead. She couldn't be dead.

Milan clutched her mom's arms, pressing her face against her chest. "No, Mommy, no."

But the only answer was the hiss of the wind over the snow.

# Chapter 16

## JANIE

# THAT KIND OF MONEY

**Three years earlier**

JANIE KNEW FRACKING WAS A WAY OF DRILLING THAT ALLOWED access to previously inaccessible oil and gas, and she had a vague mental picture of a towering drilling rig surrounded by giant storage tanks, pipelines, and other equipment.

After she poured them another cup of coffee, Steve explained to her about how oil and gas lay trapped deep in the earth, existing in secret reservoirs between layers of rock. Some smart folks had figured out that if you injected water under high pressure deep underground, it would break up—or fracture, aka frack—the bedrock. The water did the fracturing and the sand held the cracks open. The fracking fluid also contained a tiny amount of thickening agents or other chemicals to help coax out more gas.

"But what about pollution?" Janie took another bite of the banana bread she'd set out for Steve. Despite herself, she was starting to warm to the man from Prospect Power. "Isn't fracking supposed to be bad for the environment?"

Now Steve snorted. "We've got three fracking wells on our property, and we let our grandkids and our dogs run around wherever they please. Our golden retriever lived until he was fourteen and a half. If you're really worried about pollution, what we need to do is ramp up fracking and then export our gas to China. Not only will that shut down their coal mines, which just spew smoke, but it'll also provide a sustainable revenue stream for towns like ours." He pulled a face. "Besides, do you really think renewable energy is clean? Rechargeable lithium batteries depend on child labor in Congolese cobalt mines. They've got six-year-olds digging with their bare hands." As if pledging the flag, Steve put his hand on his chest. "I'm an environmentalist at heart. I also want our community and our country to be self-sufficient. I mean, what does it matter if we hit our $CO_2$ targets, if everyone is living in poverty? This job I do—it's not just about gas. It's also about raising people's standard of living."

He went on to name a long list of neighbors who'd already signed with the company. "And while Prospect can't promise they'll find anything, they're willing to pay good money to anyone who will give them a ten-year lease. If they find nothing, well, you just got yourself some free money."

Maybe Janie's luck was finally turning. After all, if you tossed a nickel into the air long enough, it couldn't keep coming up tails, year after year.

"But if Prospect does find something?" Steve leaned forward. "They'll split what they find with you. Of course, prospecting is expensive and there's a lot of up-front costs. But the royalties could still add up to a pretty penny. And tough as things sound like they are around here, that kind of money might come in pretty handy."

# Chapter 17

## MILAN

# SLEEP AND NEVER WAKE UP

MILAN HOWLED. IT STARTED LOW IN HER BELLY, SCRAPED through her chest, and scoured her throat as it was torn from her mouth. Head thrown back and eyes closed, she howled her grief and fear, her pain and rage.

But the sounds seemed to disappear as soon as they left her, sucked away by the empty mountain air. She felt as small and insubstantial as the snowflakes dotting her cheeks, disappearing on her tongue.

It was all too big. Too much. She was just a kid. And now she was an orphan. At the thought, another shriek of protest forced its way past her lips.

She was alone. In the mountains. Soon it would be dark.

Maybe she should just lie down next to her mother's body, here on the mountainside. Milan was so cold it felt like a thousand knives were cutting at every inch of exposed skin, slicing into any gap. Each breath was like inhaling glass shards.

She had read about hypothermia. As your body failed, it lied to you, told you that you were warm. That you were actually hot. Burning up. Dead people had been found frozen and naked, clothes discarded.

Milan would welcome feeling warm, even if it was a falsehood.

Still on her knees, she rested her forehead on her mom's shoulder and squeezed her eyes closed. She was exhausted. Her heart hurt. Her back hurt. Her broken finger throbbed. The leg that had been broken in the car accident ached. She wanted so badly to sleep and never wake up.

She tried to remember how to pray. At her dad's funeral, held at the little church on the hill they'd attended her whole life, she'd hoped to find the comfort she'd always felt there before. But sitting in a wheelchair next to the pew filled with her relatives, it had felt as if her prayers hadn't even gone as high as the ceiling. They had been weighed down with guilt.

Now Milan knew that guilt had been a lie, caused by someone else. The same person who had just stolen her mother from her. The same person who must now think Milan was also dead. Which would be true soon enough.

Even though her mother was as still as a marble effigy, her voice suddenly filled Milan's head.

And what it said was *Get up. Or I'll have died for nothing.*

# Chapter 18

# MILAN

# COLD AS IRON

MILAN'S FIRST PRIORITY WAS TO GET WARM, OR AT LEAST warmer. Again, she heard her mother's voice in her head.

*Get your coat.* A phrase her mom must have said a thousand times when she was a little girl.

Wincing, Milan rolled her mom's body onto one shoulder so she could take back her parka. The black polyester fabric was pocked with small shiny, brittle spots where sparks had melted it.

Milan pulled it on. For some reason, the weight and sturdiness of it made her shake even harder. What about her other clothes? This morning—had it only been this morning?—she had dressed in jeans and a T-shirt under a long-sleeved Henley. A perfectly acceptable outfit for a spring day spent inside a building or a plane, but no match for the top of a snowy mountain. She needed to subtract the jeans and add layers. The spaces between the layers would trap air, providing insulation.

She had her suitcase, but the pilot's duffel might offer additional possibilities. Maybe even a first aid kit. After closing her suitcase, she dragged it back toward the wing, her legs heavy and stiff.

Setting the pilot's duffel on the overwing door, she unzipped it. Neatly folded clothes, a silver flask, and a small brown zippered leather bag, the kind her dad had called a dopp kit. It held a razor, shaving cream, nail scissors, hair gel, toothbrush and toothpaste, floss, and a tube of sunscreen.

But no first aid kit, not even a Band-Aid.

Milan had some of the same stuff in her own 3-1-1 bag, the clear plastic one she used for liquids when she had to fly commercial. Seeing her bag in a new way, she dumped out the makeup, skin cream, and toothpaste and half filled it with snow. After zipping it closed, she folded it in half and slid it inside the sock protecting her broken finger. Now it was an ice pack. And once the snow melted, it would be water.

Her dad had always made sure they had what were called the ten essentials when they hiked. But about all Milan had from the list were extra clothes—there was no food, no map, no first aid supplies, no emergency shelter. Her phone could be a flashlight. But that was about it.

Trying not to think about the man who had once owned these things, Milan pawed through the pilot's clothes. He'd packed a couple of T-shirts, workout shorts, flannel pajama pants, a suit jacket, a belt, a pair of Nikes, socks, and underwear. Near the bottom was the prize: a pair of outdoor pants made of tightly woven polyester. Milan held them against herself. Big enough that the sweatpants she usually wore to bed could fit under them. And maybe her running tights?

Next, Milan turned to her own clothes. Clamping her chattering teeth on one side of a compression bag, she pulled it open with her good hand. The vacuum released with a sharp inhale. She shook loose the contents, then unzipped the second compression bag and added the clothes to it.

After reluctantly taking off her coat, Milan topped her Henley with a navy blue pullover and then a maroon fleece. In the heap of clothes, she spotted her oversize sweatshirt. The only time she'd worn it, Briar Woods had forced her to turn it inside out because they objected to the band named on the front. After yanking it over her head, Milan gratefully pulled the hood up over her stinging ears.

After pulling her coat back on, she stuffed a pair of socks, ready to double as mittens, in each pocket.

Next she turned her attention to her bottom half. On the door, she laid out the clothes she would replace the jeans with: her running tights, her sweatpants, and the pilot's pants. She slid her phone from her back pocket and set it next to them. In the front pocket of her jeans she felt a small rectangular lump. She pulled it out. Her lighter, the one Chance had sent her. Without it, she would never have been on the plane. Now she regarded it with new eyes. Just imagining warming her hands over a flickering fire made her shiver even harder.

She sat down on the mound of clothes and pulled off her boots, then stood up with her feet protected from the snow by one side of her open suitcase. She undid her jeans, then slid them down in one motion. While they were off, she squatted and peed, yellow on the snow. As fast as possible, she pulled on the tights, the sweatpants, and the pilot's pants. After adding a sock to replace the one around her broken finger, she pulled on a second pair and stuffed her feet into her boots.

Her shivering seemed to be lessening. Or maybe her body was just too exhausted to keep it up.

Milan checked the time on her phone. 11:47 AM. Sunset in about five hours, maybe less. She had to hurry, but she couldn't make a mistake. She slipped the phone into the back pocket of her new pants, pressing hard on the Velcro closure to make sure it caught.

What about the stuff she hadn't put on? If these clothes got wet, she'd need something dry to change into. Everything heaped on the door to the overwing locker seemed potentially useful. What if she left her toothbrush behind and her survival ended up depending on having clean teeth, or maybe sharpening the handle into a makeshift shiv?

Could she slip her arms through the duffel bag's straps and wear it like a backpack? When she lifted it, it still had heft. Something heavy was inside a closed side pocket.

After zipping it open, Milan sucked in her breath.

A gun. Cold as iron, and just as heavy.

# Chapter 19

## MILAN

# MAKE THEM PAY

MILAN RESISTED THE URGE TO FLING THE GUN AWAY FROM HER. What if it went off? Instead she carefully set it on the wing locker door.

When she tried to pull the duffel bag on like a backpack, the handles were too small. She'd have to carry it with the long strap looped over her shoulder. But after she filled the bag and took a few steps, the duffel thumped against her hip, making her feel off-balance.

*Balance.* The word made Milan think of trekking poles. They were especially useful for times when you had a heavy backpack, were going downhill, or were walking on slippery surfaces. All three of which she'd be doing soon.

What about Eric's golf clubs? Milan unzipped his bag

and pulled out two. She grabbed them by the heads, more loosely with her left hand. She took a few steps, each time stabbing the handles in the snow. With four points of contact, her footing definitely felt more secure, despite the shifting duffel bag.

She set the bag down next to the gun. When she did, the overwing door slid a few inches. Suddenly, Milan saw it in a different light. About three feet long and two feet wide, it curved up on all sides. It was smooth on the bottom except for two short fins, which presumably had something to do with being aerodynamic. Could she pull it behind her?

Milan dropped to her knees, studying it. The front had a metal eye that must have met a hook on the body of the plane when the door was closed. The opening was about as wide as her index finger. Too narrow for the pilot's belt. Floss would probably just break. What else could she use to tow it along behind her?

His Nikes! She unraveled one shoelace. It was about four feet long. Before grabbing the other shoe, she pushed the lace through the eye. Holding both ends, she gave an experimental tug. The makeshift sled glided forward.

But she needed her hands free for the golf clubs turned trekking poles. As she tied the two shoelaces together, she again thought of the pilot's belt. She could tie the shoelace to the back and then buckle it over her coat.

It worked even better than she had envisioned. Not only could she pull the sled hands-free, but the belt kept the cold air from sneaking up under her coat. Milan grinned in triumph.

But when she widened her focus, the smile fell from her face. She had miles to go through an unmarked icy wilderness. Strangers had already killed her parents, and if they learned she had survived, they would want to kill her, too. They had bombs and drones at their disposal. How was one sixteen-year-old girl supposed to survive all that?

But she didn't have a choice. She had to leave this place. Which meant she had to leave her mother. Milan gingerly tucked the gun back in the duffel. Then, stabbing the golf clubs into the snow and tugging her makeshift sled behind her, she made her way back to her mom.

Once Milan reached the body, she resolutely focused on her dad's keychain, now lying next to her mom. So many people had already died for the secrets it would unlock. Maybe she should just leave it behind. Forget her mom's instructions. Back in civilization, she could find a way to change her name and lead a normal life.

Instead she knelt next to her mom and picked up the key ring. She unzipped her coat enough to slide it into the interior chest pocket.

Still avoiding looking directly at her mom's face, Milan unbuttoned her mother's camel coat and found her small crossbody purse. Black leather, it closed with a silver sliding bolt, utilitarian and expensive-looking at the same time. She took the folded bills it held but left the credit cards, ID, lipsticks, and tiny bottle of hand sanitizer. Tucked behind everything was a photo. Milan with her mom and dad, the three of them laughing, trying to get their heads close enough over the restaurant table so the waitress could take their picture. It had been Milan's sixteenth birthday.

The tears pushed up inside her then, hot and violent, like a volcano. Swallowing hard, she forced them back down.

Before she got to her feet, she slipped the money and the photo in the same pocket as the key ring.

She was the last one left. Someone had killed her parents. Had killed Jenna and Mark and the pilot because they happened to be in the wrong place.

And now they would want to kill her.

Milan finally made herself look at her mother's face, dusted with snow. It was as lifeless as a dummy in a wax museum.

"I'll find the information and give it to Mr. Kirkby." Leaning down, she pressed her lips to her mom's ice-cold forehead before getting to her feet. "But, Mom? I'm also going to make them pay for what they did."

# Chapter 20

# JANIE
# OUT FROM UNDER

**Three years earlier**

STEVE EXPLAINED IT ALL, TALKING FAST WHILE JANIE NODDED along. Of course, there was no such thing as a perfect source of energy. Trade-offs had to be made. But drilling was a relatively painless extraction that would cause only a minor disruption. And not only would Janie be helping herself, she would be helping the US of A. Drilling for America's own natural gas was cheaper, it was theirs, and it would wean them from dependence on foreigners.

Naturally, there would be a little initial disturbance, a bit more traffic, a few trucks, some noise from drilling. But it wouldn't be long before that part was over. The grass would grow back and so would the trees. The new gravel access roads would be lightly used, just to get to the well-heads. Every now and then a man would look in to see how things were going.

Janie nodded, her hands wrapped around her coffee cup. What Steve said made sense. The NIMBYs might complain. But once the drilling started and they saw how it was really done, they would shut up. Nothing important would change.

And Janie could finally get out from under that pile of debt.

Chapter 21

## MILAN
# FIND HER BONES

BOOTS CRUNCHING IN THE SNOW, MILAN SET OFF DOWNHILL. SHE was heading in the direction of the dark line of water she'd spotted from up in the tree. The trees were spaced apart enough that she could walk between them. To ensure she kept moving in the right direction, she picked out three trees that led in the direction she wanted to go, and lined them up, one behind another. When she reached the first tree, she picked out a new one, farther down the mountain, that lined up with the remaining two. The snow had tapered off, making it easier to see. Most of the trees had tall straight trunks like telephone poles, with branches that didn't start until about twenty feet up. Only a few had limbs that started near the ground. It was lucky that she'd been able to climb the tree with the wing.

Lucky! The thought made Milan shake her head. Nothing about this was lucky.

The door turned sled grazed her ankles with every step as the shoelace tugged it forward. Twenty minutes ago, using it had seemed like such a clever idea. But maybe it would be better to abandon the door and deal with the duffel bag throwing her off-balance.

She came to a spot where the hill made a short, steep dip. After stabbing the ends of the golf clubs into the snow, Milan started to clamber down.

This time, the door swept her feet out from under her.

With a shriek, she landed flat on her back, on top of the duffel bag. The door kept moving. When she tried to stop it, the club in her left hand caught on some underbrush. It bent her broken finger backward when it was wrenched out of her grasp.

The wing locker's door had become a runaway bobsled. It was moving faster than her thoughts could catch up. The only thing left in her head was the sensation of sliding, the branches flickering overhead.

And suddenly Milan was eight, during one of Portland's rare snowfalls, sledding with Chance down a steep hill in their neighborhood park. If you weren't careful, by the time you reached the bottom, you might build up so much momentum that you just kept going, sailing right out into the street. Every snowstorm, fourth-hand stories were repeated about how some kid had been hit by a car after doing exactly that.

Back then, the potential danger had made sledding even more exciting. Now, as Milan snapped her attention back to the present, all the possible ways this could end seemed terrifying.

Keeping a tight grip on the remaining golf club, Milan managed to sit up, scooting back and raising her knees to her chest so her feet didn't catch in the snow. Although when she was a kid, that was how she had steered her toboggan. With her feet. To steer to the left, you put your left foot into the snow. To go right, you did the opposite. And to stop, you put down both feet and used your heels as brakes.

Her toboggan had had a rope she could pull to raise up the front while using her weight on the back of the sled as an additional brake. All Milan had now was a shoelace that went behind her back, between her legs, and through the eyebolt.

And back then, even on the steepest part of that big hill, she had never gone as fast as she was going now. Gingerly, she stuck out her feet and slowly lowered her boots. With a high-pitched chattering sound, they skittered over the snow. She tried to dig in her heels, but the door was sliding downhill so fast it was hard to find any purchase. And what if she pushed too deep? She might snap an ankle. Then she would slowly freeze to death, lost among the trees of this endless snowy forest. With luck, in the summer some hiker would find her bones.

But she couldn't just leave the sled to its own devices. Sooner or later she was going to run into something. At high speed. Her teeth were rattling. Her vision was bouncing and blurring.

Gritting her teeth, Milan forced her feet down, plowing them deeper, keeping her toes upturned. Her boots sent up a spray of white snow that stung her face. But she still wasn't stopping. She was barely slowing down.

She raised her gaze. Directly in her path, about three hundred feet ahead, was a huge tree with a broad trunk. With a grunt of effort, Milan dug in her left foot and leaned hard to the left.

Somehow she missed the tree. But she had overcommitted. The door tipped even as it slowed from going against the grain of the hill. Milan hit the ground hard and slid, the snow exploding up around her. The impact crushed the breath out of her lungs.

And then everything was still. The forest. Her breath. Even her heart.

# Chapter 22

LENNY

# MORE REAL THAN ANYTHING

YOU HIRED LENNY WHEN YOU WANTED THINGS DONE WITH finesse. With a certain sense of style. And sometimes when you wanted to send a message.

Two years ago, when a midwestern governor had started advocating for greater oversight of fracking, Lenny had hacked into the guy's emails. Ostentatiously religious, the governor was the type who wouldn't be caught dead with anything more interesting than a box of Cheez-Its. And yet Lenny had gotten photos of him with a blond, a woman who was most definitely not the wife he squired to church each Sunday. Confronted with the evidence, the governor had acted rationally.

Seven months ago, a water quality scientist named Floyd Higgins had become an example for anyone who might be thinking of running their mouth. He was the victim of a freak accident involving a misstep down his basement stairs, the concrete floor at the bottom, and the two long days before anyone found him. But Floyd had lived. He'd lived badly: broken legs, a crushed pelvis, cracked ribs, and a smashed jaw. He spent weeks in intensive care and would be in a wheelchair for the rest of his life. But he had learned to stop talking about the damage all that unregulated fracking was doing.

After hacking into the lab's computers, Lenny had wiped clean all the data he had collected. But she suspected one loose end had escaped and found its way to Senator Jack Mayhew. Right before Floyd's accident, the senator had received a package with no return address. It contained only a thumb drive. After he saw what was on it, Jack had begun making discreet inquiries. When they attracted attention, he refused to listen to reason. Refused to be bribed. Refused to be threatened.

So he had to be silenced.

Lenny had designed the hit on Jack to look like an accident. It was chalked up to a narrow road, speed limits that were routinely exceeded, and an overworked man who had drifted into the other lane. Investigators believed the other driver must have been distracted, too, probably because the Honda they were driving was stolen. After briefly stopping and rendering first aid to the senator's daughter, the driver had fled the scene. The only description authorities had was of a guy of average height and weight, dressed in a dark hoodie and jeans.

Lenny. Lenny was good at being the person that people never quite focused on.

For several months, she thought she'd succeeded. But then a few weeks ago, Jack's wife, Heather, had started asking the same questions. And so she had had to be silenced as well.

Yes, others had died, including the pilot and the girl whose life Lenny had saved only a few months ago. But it was the same when a surgeon cut out a tumor. To be sure they got it all, they also had to excise a certain amount of healthy tissue surrounding it. And sometimes even that wasn't enough. She knew that firsthand.

It wouldn't take authorities long to figure out it hadn't been a bird strike or a catastrophic engine failure. But even if parts of the bomb survived, she had made sure they were generic. Untraceable. Without a single fingerprint whorl.

Not that her prints were on file.

Unlike in Karl's day, now it wasn't enough to just take someone out. The clients, especially this one, liked proof. A slick video. A montage of forbidden embraces or devouring flames or an unsuspecting diner doubling over, clawing his throat. Perhaps a focus on a person drawing his last bubbling breath. Or in this case, a still figure lying on the snow.

Once back in her hotel room, Lenny uploaded the camera card to her laptop and set to work, a cup of coffee at her elbow. She edited it down to the best shots, already thinking about the classical music it could ultimately be set to. The drone footage of Heather's demise was much more cinematic than the dash cam footage of Jack's car accident had been.

The flyover shot of the forest. The reveal shot as the drone rose up over the trees to unveil the scattered wreckage. Followed by the aerial pan from a hover. And finally the close-up shot of a dead Heather.

As Lenny trimmed and rearranged, a cough bubbled up, but she suppressed it. Stupid thing had been hanging on for weeks.

She had watched all these events in real time a few hours ago, but only on the pixelated 1080p version beamed back to the iPad. Comparing those to the images captured by the Hasselblad camera was like the passage from Corinthians that Lenny's mom had liked: "For now we see through a glass, darkly; but then face to face." What the camera had filmed seemed more real than anything in this anonymous room.

And now Lenny was able to see two things that hadn't been clear on the iPad.

Even though Heather had lain so still, as still as the dead, her nostrils had flared the tiniest amount each time she breathed. Because that was what she had been doing three hours ago.

Breathing.

And leading away from her body toward the trees were marks. Faint but there.

Footprints.

# Chapter 23

MILAN
# DESPITE EVERYTHING

IN THE HUSHED STILLNESS OF THE FOREST, MILAN LAY SPRAWLED on her side, her left cheek pressed against the snow. Her mouth opened and closed like a fish yanked from the water, but air refused to either enter or leave her lungs. After everything that had happened today, she couldn't summon the energy to panic about her inability to breathe. Eventually she was able to take a tiny sip of air. The next one was a little bigger. She rolled onto her back, knees bent, and closed her eyes.

In her mind's eye, Milan saw herself and Chance, eight years old again. As clearly as if it had just happened, she remembered the time her sled had bucked them sideways, overturning the two of them into a snowdrift. They had laughed, digging their way to freedom with their gloved hands.

And suddenly Milan's chest completely loosened as the spasm in her diaphragm ended. In less than twenty-four hours, everything had been stripped away from her. Her school, her mother, her sense of safety. She took a long, deep breath. Whoever had bombed the plane had done their best to kill her. But here she was. Still alive, despite everything.

Thanks to the pilot's shoelaces, the makeshift sled had ended up next to her, like a board tethered to a surfer. After sending up a silent thank-you to Nike for making strong shoelaces, Milan sat up. She couldn't spot the golf club that had been wrenched from her hands, and she decided not to waste precious time and energy trying to find it. The duffel was about fifteen feet away, and the remaining golf club was back where she had turned. After retrieving them, Milan turned the door over and set them down.

Her footsteps crunched. The bootprints might reveal her presence if the drone returned. When she looked back the way she had come, a few scuffs marked where she had tried to slow herself down, but the trail her makeshift sled had left was very faint.

Her broken finger no longer throbbed. She flexed her hand experimentally. It still moved but felt completely numb. Was that a good thing or a bad thing? She pulled off the sock turned mitten. The ice pack had melted, leaving the 3-1-1 bag half-filled with water. Water! She undid the zipper an inch and tilted her head back. It was icy, refreshing, and not nearly enough. After refilling the bag with snow, she wrapped her hand around it and pulled the sock back over everything.

Milan spun the belt around her waist so the shoelace was in front, then settled back down on top of the duffel with the golf club tucked at her side. Planting a foot on either side, she pushed. She held on to the shoelace with both hands to provide a point of balance.

Slowly Milan picked up speed. But she was able to keep the rate manageable, turning and braking as the terrain required. A few times a thick stand of trees meant she had to pick up the sled and detour around them. To avoid going in circles, she alternated going to the left and to the right. She hadn't found the stream yet, but it didn't seem like it could be too far away. And then she would follow the water to civilization.

A little laugh escaped her lips. She was doing it. She was doing the impossible.

Directly ahead of her was an evergreen that looked like a Christmas tree. It sat on top of the snow, branches brushing the ground. She pressed her right heel into the snow so she could flank it. But then her boot caught something, a rocky outcropping or a broken branch, that sent her tumbling off her sled and toward the tree trunk.

As Milan plunged headfirst into loose snow, she realized the tree was more like an iceberg.

And she had only seen the tip.

# Chapter 24

## MILAN
# RAGGED SNARLING

THE EVERGREEN WAS MUCH TALLER THAN IT HAD SEEMED. WHAT Milan had thought was snow-covered ground was actually a mix of additional branches and loose snow. Like an umbrella, the dense branches higher up had caught most of the snow. What sifted through had not been packed down by the weight of continued accumulation, the way it would have been out in the open.

Milan panicked. But the more she thrashed, the more she kicked and twisted, the deeper she sank into the powdery stuff. The merciless snow pressed in on all sides. She was completely submerged.

She recognized what this was. A tree well. Two years ago, a snowboarder from her school had fallen into one and had been smothered to death. It was like quicksand, only made of ice crystals.

And if Milan remembered anything from watching old TV shows, the way to get out of quicksand was paradoxical: to stop fighting. So for a long moment, she forced herself to lie still as she tried to slow her breathing. The faster she breathed, the faster whatever air was trapped with her would be used up.

She coughed, clearing the snow from her mouth. Slowly, slowly, she forced her hands up toward her face, trying to clear a bigger pocket of air in front of it. Her heart was rabbiting in her chest.

Her instinct was to curl up in a ball to protect herself. Instead she needed to make herself as flat and horizontal as possible, to distribute her weight evenly across the snow.

But what *was* horizontal? When she tumbled into this ocean of snow, she had lost her bearings. Milan needed to get back out into the air, but what direction was that? Were her feet over her head? Was she face up or face down? She had no idea. The shoelace went from the belt at her waist and between her legs. It felt like the overwing door was above her, but did that mean the air was as well? The unpacked snow had swallowed up both of them with ease.

The panic built up again. To keep it at bay, she took a slightly longer sip of air. The white that pressed in around her did not seem brighter in any direction. But if she tunneled the wrong way, she would suffocate.

Suddenly she thought of her dad's advice again, but in a different way. Water flowed downhill. If she spit, gravity would show her which way was down—and in the opposite direction would be light and air.

Milan chewed her dry tongue, trying to work up some moisture. Finally, she collected it in the front of her mouth and spit. The spit dropped straight down from her lips to the other side of her air pocket.

Okay. So she was face down, her feet a little higher than her head. Using a rocking motion, Milan rested her weight on her elbows, pushed her shoulders up, and tried to grow her air pocket. Even though the air entering her lungs felt like it was growing thinner, she ordered herself to stay calm and move slowly. Going against every instinct, she next pressed herself down evenly. This both distributed her weight and compacted the snow. With each small adjustment, she slowly moved her head a little higher.

Even if she managed to get herself oriented toward the sky, if she tried to dig her way up, the snow would just fall back on top of her. But what if she went sideways? If she could get out from under the branches, the snow would be firmer.

Milan swam her arms to the right, always keeping a shoulder in front of her mouth, preventing it from filling with snow. At the same time, she scissored her legs sideways. The belt cut into her waist and the shoelace sawed at her inner thigh as she forced the sled to move with her.

Slowly, slowly, her modified snow angel move worked, allowing the snow to support her as she moved out from underneath the tree. Finally when she reached out her socked hand, it touched a branch. Milan gripped it and pulled. Once she was closer, she hooked her right knee and elbow over it. Grunting, she kept narrowing the distance, until finally she felt the press of the branch from her sternum to her crotch. With her last bit of grit, Milan managed to push herself up.

Her head popped out into the crisp, fresh air. It was sharp and cold, the sweetest pain.

# Chapter 25

## LENNY
# TAKE ADVANTAGE

KARL, LENNY'S DAD, HAD MADE IT A POINT TO NEVER SWEAR.
Uttering an epithet, even if you were alone, he firmly
believed, could reveal your weak points.

But if ever there was a good time to swear, it was now.
Nothing was going to plan. A not-quite-dead Senator
Heather Mayhew was definitely not what the client had
paid for. And equally bad, who had left those faint footprints leading away from her body?

With gritted teeth, Lenny had examined the drone
footage of the surrounding forest frame by frame, zooming
in on any anomaly. As the drone flew back, it had passed
over the tree holding the plane's wing. It was hard to spot,
but about halfway up, pressed against the trunk, hidden

under the branches, had been a dark shape. A person dressed in black, head tilted down? Lenny thought so.

Someone who foolishly thought of themselves as a survivor.

Lenny changed before heading out. Now the engine of the Subaru Outback—Oregon's unofficial state car, and thus basically invisible—surged as it negotiated another backroad curve. A black bag on the passenger seat held the drone, the controller, the iPad, and, this time, the laptop. Never make the same mistake twice, as Karl would say.

Lenny parked again on the old logging road and sent the drone back up. On the iPad, she watched the forest as the drone skimmed over it, looking for a loose end and finding none. In ten minutes, the drone was once again hovering over Heather. She didn't appear to have shifted from her position since. With the temperatures hovering in the low twenties, surely that was a death sentence. When the drone returned, Lenny would still check to be sure.

In the intervening time, the other mystery had only deepened. The initial footage had shown a faint line of footprints leading away from Heather toward the tree holding the wing.

Now the wing was on the ground. The wing locker was open, contents strewn about. Clearly someone had survived, at least for a while.

And the footprints had multiplied. They led from

Heather to the wing and back again. Lenny slowly moved the drone over them. The size was uniform. It looked like a single person had made the roundtrip journey between Heather and the wing at least twice. Then, starting from the body, the prints set off in a new direction, down the mountain, roughly southwest.

With the drone, Lenny followed those prints, squinting at the iPad. It had to be a trick of the wintery light. Because it looked like they just stopped, as if whoever it was had simply disappeared.

Which wasn't possible.

So who had made them? Lenny's money was on the pilot. Ex-military. Multiple tours. Known to be discreet. He'd managed to bring the plane down more or less intact, which already meant Lenny had underestimated what he was capable of.

Had he managed to jump up into a tree at the point the footprints disappeared? But none seemed close enough. And why would he?

No matter who it was, how long could they stay alive? How many miles could you get in the mountains with no food, no shelter, no map, no cell service, and with nighttime temperatures dipping into the teens? Survival would be all but impossible. Even for ex-military. Even for someone like Karl, who had survived three assassination attempts.

Lenny wished for an infrared camera but didn't dwell on the oversight. You worked with what you had, which in this case was a drone and weak light. It was time for it to come back to base.

While the drone was returning, tires crunched down the cutoff. Lenny tossed the controller on the seat and quickly pulled the bag over it, hiding it.

"Ma'am?" A man said behind Lenny. "Ma'am, are you all right?"

Lenny turned, her fingertips resting on the butt of her concealed gun.

"Oh, yeah." She bit her lip, looked shyly downward. "The baby just shifted and put a lot of pressure on my bladder. I had to pull over."

Wearing a parka and a beanie, the guy was about her age, late thirties, with an already weather-beaten face. He regarded her with narrowed eyes, considering.

Lenny almost hoped he would see her as someone to take advantage of. As prey.

She wanted to kill someone so badly right now.

# Chapter 26

## MILAN

# JUST FOR A SECOND

THE SHADOWS WERE LENGTHENING, AND MILAN STILL HADN'T found the stream. Now she needed it twice over. Not only could it lead her to civilization, but more immediately it would ease her thirst. She'd again drunk melted snow from her 3-1-1 bag, but her body cried out for more. Her tongue felt thick.

Milan was now pulling the door behind her instead of trying to ride on top of it. She'd already gotten lucky twice. It wouldn't happen a third time.

It didn't seem like it would be safe to keep moving once it was fully dark, even if she wasted battery by using her phone as a flashlight. But she didn't think she could sleep without having more to drink. And at least moving generated heat.

Milan's whole body hurt, from her pounding head to her aching toes. Her face felt chapped and raw. It was harder and harder to lift her boots from the snow.

She looked back the way she had come. In the light of the setting sun, the snowcapped mountain was an unnatural orange. The light played tricks, making her think of claws, jagged and sharp, about to close around her.

Milan hadn't been alone this long in quite some time. At all three boarding schools there had been at least one roommate. Farting. Snoring. Chattering away, even when she had her earbuds in. Asking for help with homework or gossiping about other students. The more she'd been surrounded by other people, the more alone she'd felt.

But now that Milan was truly alone, she longed to be able to communicate. A look, a laugh, even a text. Someone to cheer her on, to offer her reassurance. She imagined what it would be like to have Chance by her side, how they would debate about what to do next. Instead all she had was the occasional sound of her own voice, commenting on her surroundings, repeating advice she remembered her parents giving, or speaking directly to them, telling them how much she loved them.

The afternoon was sliding into night. The sound of water broke through her trance. A dark slash in the white, it was about three feet wide, with two-foot-high banks of snow.

At the sight, her mouth flooded with saliva. But if she crouched on the bank to get to the water, it might crumble beneath her. She couldn't afford to fall in. Even with the lighter, there was no way to start a fire, not without fuel and a dry space to set it up on.

Finally she lay on her belly and squirmed forward until she could reach the surface of the water with outstretched hands. She pulled the socks turned mittens from her hands. When she dipped the empty bag in, the water was so cold at first her brain registered it as scalding hot. After scooting back from the stream, Milan got to her knees, tilted the bag back, and took a long swallow.

The icy water was far colder than the melted snow had been. Her diaphragm spasmed. It felt like someone had stabbed her in the breastbone with an icicle. She dropped the bag, pressed her hand under her chest, and doubled over. The agony pushed out all other thoughts.

Slowly, the pain eased to a dull ache. She forced herself to get more water and then warmed it, one mouthful at a time, before swallowing. Finally she put the socks back over her hands and got to her feet. She wanted nothing more than to lie down and sleep.

No. That wasn't true. There were things Milan wanted more than sleep. To live. And to avenge her parents' deaths.

She walked downstream, keeping well back from the bank. The world was turning black and white, the color leached away by the fading light. As soon as the last bit of glow disappeared from the horizon, it would be all black. She couldn't go any farther, but she also couldn't sleep sprawled on the snow. Maybe she'd have to sleep standing up, like the main character in Hans Christian Andersen's *The Little Match Girl*.

Finally, she spotted two trees growing about three feet apart. Even though they were the kind with long trunks, Milan still tested each step with the golf club to make sure it wouldn't give way beneath her.

After wedging the door between the trees, she opened the duffel bag. She laid down one of the empty compression bags to provide some insulation, topping it with one of the pilot's T-shirts. Using her good hand and her teeth, she split the bottom seam on the other compression bag, then slipped her boots through the short, narrow tube. It only came up to her knees, but it would keep the bottom part of her legs dry. The rest of the clothes she wrapped and layered around herself. Her face felt chapped, so she rubbed sunscreen on it. After filling the 3-1-1 bag with snow again, she tucked it into the sock protecting her hand. She put the nearly empty duffel bag under her butt.

Her last step was to knot the neck of the pilot's other T-shirt. Then with her hood still up, she pulled the T-shirt over her head until it was stopped by the knot. Wiggling like someone in a straitjacket, she pulled it down to her elbows. It was like a tiny tent, and almost immediately filled with warmth and moisture from her exhalations.

Then Milan folded herself up on top of the duffel bag. Her back pressed against one trunk and the toes of her boots against the other. After crossing her arms on her bent knees, she leaned forward.

Milan knew she wouldn't really be able to sleep. Which was probably for the best.

Still, she closed her eyes, just for a second.

Chapter 27

JANIE
# JUST THE BEGINNING

**Three years earlier**

PROSPECT POWER'S FIRST OFFER WAS FOR $250 AN ACRE. JANIE
hesitated, especially since Becca had heard rumors down
at the restaurant about people getting more. A few weeks
later, it jumped to $1,000 an acre. It seemed too good to be
true. It was life-changing money. For a ten-year lease on
their 146 acres, they would get $146,000.

Janie talked it over with Becca and Thad, and they all
agreed it was a godsend. Never before had she had that
much money at one time. She paid the property tax, settled
the bill at the feed store, and bought a nearly new tractor to
replace the one that kept breaking down. She got an electric oven, and new clothes for the kids. She was thinking

about getting a new-to-her used truck. Or maybe even putting a down payment on one of those robot milkers.

And this could just be the beginning. Janie was hearing they were finding gas on nearby properties. Her neighbor Arlen Brandeis had gone to Hawaii with his wife, where he had worn shorts and sandals for the first time in his life.

Everyone was benefiting. Becca's hours at the restaurant had gone to full-time. The pay Prospect Power offered was so good that even Thad had started working for them, driving a pumper truck. The town had gone from sleepy to booming, with industry trucks and large pickups jamming the single main street to the point where you couldn't take a left turn. Throughout the valley, new restaurants and hotels had sprung up to service the rig and pipeline workers.

Prospect Power was putting money back into the community: sponsoring fireworks shows, donating money for picnics, and helping out the police and fire departments. They were even hosting the Oil Baron's Ball, a black-tie affair, to raise funds for the arts, and Becca was trying to talk Thad into going.

The future was looking bright.

# Chapter 28

# LENNY
## ODDLY PERSONAL

LENNY LAY IN THE HOTEL BED BUT COULDN'T SLEEP. SHE TRIED TO tell herself it was all the coffee she had drunk but knew it wasn't true.

At least she no longer had to worry about Heather. The second senator Mayhew was truly dead. The new footage from the drone had confirmed it. While she might have been sort of dead a few hours earlier, by late afternoon she had been 100 percent dead. Even in the 5.1K version.

As for the guy who had almost caught her with the drone, Lenny had let him go. Let him live. If he remembered anything about her, it would be her pregnancy and her dirty-blond hair. Both of them fake. Besides, a dead guy a few miles from the site of a bombed airplane would have raised more questions than the brief satisfaction of dispatching him was worth.

Right now, no one knew what had happened to Heather and the others on the plane. Her staff must be starting to wonder, but Lenny hadn't seen anything on the channels she was monitoring.

A few hours ago, a commercial jetliner cruising at thirty-two thousand feet had reported picking up an emergency locator transmitter but had been unable to get a fix on its location. When the aircraft controller used a computer program to plot a potential search area, it had been far too wide to be useful, encompassing Oregon, Washington, Montana, and Idaho.

As she tried to contort the hotel pillow into a more comfortable shape, Lenny decided there was no point in telling the client Heather had lived for a bit. A few deft cuts, some filter adjustments for the different ways the light fell, and the client could still receive a beautifully presented video of Heather paying the price for asking too many questions.

Karl would have rolled his eyes at the client's requests. Maybe she should take a lesson from her father and be less accommodating.

Karl had loved only one thing in the world. Lenny.

Well, Lenny and cigarettes.

And in return, Lenny had loved him.

According to Karl, he had taken Lenny on her first job when she was three months old. Strapped to his chest in a BabyBjörn. Then Karl pulled out the gun hidden underneath the dark blue quilted fabric. The victim was not the kind who would carry a weapon himself, so Karl hadn't been worried about her being injured.

As Lenny got older, providing a distraction or helping her dad surveil was a game, one she excelled at. She lived for his infrequent smile. He didn't take her on all his jobs, but whenever he did, no one expected a killer to have a kid in tow.

Lenny had been homeschooled. That's what Karl told the state. In addition to math and English, he also taught her what he'd learned in the military as well as everything he had taught himself. With a cigarette continually tucked in the corner of his mouth, he'd shown Lenny how to evade surveillance, create improvised weapons, pick locks, get out of handcuffs, read maps, and speak enough Spanish, Chinese, and German to be useful. From Karl, Lenny learned how to shoot a gun, throw a knife, make a bomb, and use every part of her body as a weapon.

Some fathers took their kids out hunting. Karl had done the same, only their targets had been people. Lenny had made her first hit when she was thirteen.

Her father had been a sociopath, Lenny knew that now. When Karl was on a job, he easily slipped into new roles, because he had been acting all his life. Acting as if he were like everyone else. Karl didn't really feel sadness or joy. Most emotions were foreign to him, something he could think about intellectually but not experience. He felt fascination. Envy, sometimes. Desire. Life was a game, and his goal was to win it. If there was something he wanted, he would do what was necessary to get it.

Karl liked being powerful. And what was more powerful than deciding how and when someone should die?

Lenny and Karl had the same straight brown hair and pale blue eyes. Anyone who saw them together remarked on the resemblance. Him loving Lenny had been the same as loving himself. Or as close to love as he could get. By the time Lenny figured out how twisted it all was, it was too late. She had been shaped by him.

It would certainly be easier to be like Karl. Sometimes when she saw the fear in her target's eyes, Lenny hesitated. Just a little.

Over time, Karl admitted Lenny had advantages he didn't. No matter how easily he smiled, how good a backstory he constructed, people were a little on edge around him. Even when he looked the part, he wasn't quite the chameleon he wanted to be. But when Lenny faked an emotion, it was still one she had actually felt before.

And being a woman had its advantages. A woman blended in. A woman was considered more trustworthy. How many mothers had told their children if they got lost to ask a woman for help? And women didn't make men nervous. If anything, they thought a woman had something to fear from them.

Why hire a meat mountain if you wanted someone who no one would look at twice? Lenny looked like someone's wife, someone's mom. Like the server who brought you your drink, the clerk who handed you the form, the distracted driver who had just bumped your fender.

Lenny could be forgettable. Or, if required, she drew attention to herself. Once, she had spent five weeks rescuing stray cats, dressing in colorful scarves, and painting street scenes from the balcony of her new apartment—an apartment that just happened to have a clear view of the target's penthouse suite across the street. She had seemed harmless and a little eccentric.

Until she wasn't.

Or maybe the role called for beauty. With the right makeup and clothing, you couldn't take your eyes off Lenny. She might accompany a target back to his hotel room, where he'd be found the next morning with a faked prescription bottle on the bedside table.

You called Lenny when you wanted to solve a human problem. Basically, she was a hit man. She had snorted when one of her clients had tried to call her a hit person.

On paper, she was a self-employed IT consultant who sometimes had to travel for work. No one ever asked too many questions, and if they did, she just enthusiastically spouted jargon until their eyes glazed.

If you wanted a professional, you paid—and paid well. It wasn't like Lenny needed to kill someone every hour, forty hours a week. She could go weeks or even months in between gigs. Her targets were businesspeople, nosy politicians, or those who had come into possession of things—including knowledge—they shouldn't have.

Lenny never got involved in situations where someone wanted a family member dead. Too messy, too personal.

But this job was breaking every one of her unwritten rules. Far too messy. And oddly personal.

# Chapter 29

MILAN

# WHAT SHE WOULD DO

MILAN STARTLED AWAKE. HER DREAMS HAD BEEN FILLED WITH the sounds of a woman screaming. High-pitched, wordless, ululating.

She opened her eyes. Nothing but darkness. The world was as black as the inside of her eyelids. Had she gone blind?

She almost screamed herself before she remembered the knotted T-shirt she'd pulled over her head before falling asleep. Last night, she had welcomed the warmth of her own exhaled breath filling the little cone of fabric. Now it felt like she was suffocating. She tore it off. Parts were stiff with ice, and new snow had fallen overnight and mounded on top of her head and shoulders.

The sun hadn't yet risen but the eastern edge of the sky was lighter.

Milan pulled the compression bag off her lower legs. Despite two pairs of socks, her hands were stiff and numb, especially her left one with the broken finger. Unfolding her legs, she pushed herself to her feet. Like water going down a drain, the world began to swirl. She plopped back down on the duffel bag and waited for everything to stop spinning.

Earlier, the cold had seemed like an outside force. Now it felt like it had slipped inside, turning her bones to ice, filling her chest. Each beat of her heart drove the cold deeper into her veins.

This time when she got to her feet, Milan put her palms on one of the trees for balance. Her boots sank into the fresh snow.

She tried to pace, to force the blood back into her toes, but the new snow made it difficult. She switched to stomping her feet in place. The bone in her leg that had been broken in the car accident throbbed.

The sun peeked over the mountain, revealing a pristine, white world, so bright she had to squint. Behind her, her tracks had disappeared. Right now, no one knew she was here. No one knew she was even alive. And according to her mother, that was a good thing.

Leave no trace, her dad used to say as he plucked other people's discarded granola bar wrappers or old chip bags from the trail to pack out. That made her remember how he'd always brought plenty of snacks when they hiked. Gorp. Nuts. M&M's, if real bribery might be needed.

Yesterday morning at school, Milan had barely eaten, too nervous about what her mom would say. She'd only managed to choke down a cup of coffee and a couple of forkfuls of scrambled eggs. Now she imagined sinking her teeth into a toasted bagel slick with butter. Drinking a glass of orange juice, the color so saturated it almost glowed. Dishing up a big bowl of oatmeal, and then topping it with whole milk, brown sugar, walnuts, and slices of banana. Her stomach rumbled.

Her dad had talked about the rule of threes for survival. Three minutes without air, three days without water, three weeks without food. So supposedly she could last another two weeks and six days without eating. In the school before last, a battered paperback copy of *Alive* had been passed from hand to hand as each student in turn marveled at or was grossed out by the true story of the rugby team forced to resort to cannibalism after their plane crashed in the Andes.

Milan was hungry, but she would never be *that* hungry.

Food was the least of her problems. Maybe that was why it was so beguiling. No matter how much she thought about her parents, she would never see them again. But with luck, in a few hours she might be able to eat.

She pulled the sock on her left hand back to get at her 3-1-1 bag, and slurped the water from it. Then Milan unwound the sock from the rest of her hand and regarded her broken finger. It was a rainbow of colors, so swollen the wrinkles on her knuckle were turned inside out, puffing up instead of folding in.

Milan took stock. She was cold. She was hungry and thirsty. She was lost in the woods. Her broken finger throbbed, her ribs ached, her neck was stiff, and every muscle protested. She was bruised and battered, emotionally as well as physically.

None of that was going to kill her. At least not today.

But whoever had murdered her parents might be looking for her, or would be if they realized her body wasn't on the plane. What if they were in these mountains right now, using that drone to hunt her down?

She and her dad had done a few fifteen-mile day hikes. Even if she could only do half that distance today, it might still be enough to take her to some kind of civilization.

Her plan to follow the stream made sense, but what would she do once she met someone else?

Milan touched her phone, smooth and cold, tucked in the back pocket of pants that had belonged to a man who was now dead.

What should she do once she had service?

# Chapter 30

## LENNY
# TARGETS, NOT VICTIMS

LENNY HAD DREAMED KARL WAS SITTING IN THE CHAIR AT THE end of her hotel bed, next to the blank black screen of the TV, watching her. Even after Lenny opened her eyes and saw the empty chair, she could still picture Karl's flat eyes and yellow-stained fingertips. Smell the woodsy, harsh smoke. Hear the soft crackle of the paper as it burned a bit further with each inhalation. In her dream, he had been blowing smoke out the side of his mouth.

Sometimes Karl would light the next cigarette with the cherry of the one he was finishing. Soda or beer cans always made the best ashtrays. Lenny had learned to be careful. If she picked up a can she thought was hers and took a swig, she might end up with a mouthful of smoker's dregs. Karl would just laugh as she gagged and spit.

If Karl were really here, what advice would he give her? He wouldn't tell her she had messed up. After all, she had done what she was paid to do. Killed Senator Heather Mayhew. The question was, what had happened between the time the plane crashed and when Heather died?

Sometimes things didn't go according to plan. That's when you stepped in with a new plan. Karl had taught Lenny there were a million ways to kill someone, limited only by your ingenuity. Guns, knives, poison, ice picks, tire irons, baseball bats, switched medications, a pillow over the face, your hands around their neck. And, of course, bombs.

As Lenny got up and started heating water in the in-room coffee maker, she remembered the first time she had used a bomb she had built herself. It had been exhilarating. She'd been dressed from head to toe in black, riding a motorcycle with no plates on the 101. The helmet had made her anonymous, androgynous. Caught in one of LA's frequent backups, she'd taken advantage of the law allowing motorcyclists to split lanes. After jockeying for space with the target's limousine, she had slapped the magnetic bomb on the passenger-side door, accompanying it with a gesture implying the car had gotten too close.

Then Lenny zoomed off before the bodyguards could

think things through. A block later, she pressed a button. Afterward, she'd disappeared into a maze of streets. Meanwhile her target was dead and she'd just made enough cash that she didn't need to work for at least six months.

Karl had taught her to think of them as targets, not victims. And since Lenny had no connection to them, it was hard for the authorities to tease out what had happened.

It didn't matter how many protective measures a target took, there were always vulnerabilities if you looked. Everyone had a weak spot: a medical condition, a bad habit, an allergy, or a favorite place, activity, or person. Basically, they were human.

And humans liked routines. Routines were a great way to save mental energy. Routines helped people be productive.

Routines got people killed.

The last of the hot water sputtered into the cup. Lenny would rather brew dirt than drink the hotel's free coffee. Instead she poured the hot water into the AeroPress she'd brought, along with some freshly ground beans. She was a sucker for gadgets. At home, she had an Instant Pot, a Brava countertop oven that cooked with pulses of light, and a blowtorch she mostly used for caramelizing sugar.

Mostly.

When she was on a job, Lenny liked to have a gun in an ankle holster and another at the small of her back. On her keychain was a Kubotan. She had another in her purse, disguised as a pen—and that could actually write. She didn't buy the crap they sold at the so-called spy stores. Lenny got the more serious versions, but she still got them.

Now she stirred the coffee sludge with the wide Aero-Press stirrer stick, removed it, then pressed the plunger down with both hands. It required enough pressure that she had to layer one palm on top of the other, just like trying to stop bleeding.

While Lenny drank the coffee—black, no sugar—she checked her laptop. Late last night, Heather's staff had reported that she hadn't shown, but as of yet, there were only questions and no answers.

She returned again to the question that had caused her such restless sleep. Who besides Heather had survived, and for how long? Because whoever it was, they had to be dead by now.

Right?

So who had survived the crash? Eric, Jenna, Mark, Milan, or the pilot, Maury?

Eric was soft. Used to his comforts. Jenna was fashion obsessed, a social climber. A pretty, petty party girl. It was hard to imagine her turning into some kind of wilderness survival expert. Mark, Heather's legislative director, might have had the temperament, but he was in his late sixties. Milan was a kid with pins holding one of her legs together.

With his military background, Maury was the only logical choice. But really, how far could he get?

To tell the client or not to tell the client, that was the question. And just like Hamlet's plaintive query, it concerned life itself. Because there was more than one Lenny out there. And if the client learned the truth, he might just hire someone else to clean up this mess. Take care of Lenny as well as whoever had survived the plane crash.

Coffee finished, she took a shower, brushed her teeth, strapped on her weapons, and got dressed. By the time she checked her laptop again, the outside world was starting to fit the pieces together. The emergency signal picked up the afternoon before. Senator Mayhew's missing plane. Authorities had already determined the senator's daughter had boarded in Colorado, and that the pilot had been flying from there to Portland by visual flight rules. Even without a flight plan on file, that had narrowed things down considerably.

A new alert popped up. Ten minutes ago, a US Air Force flyover had spotted some wreckage. Now authorities were debating whether to send in snowmobiles or a helicopter or some combination. Not for rescue, but recovery. As Lenny had originally thought, they seemed to believe everyone on board was dead.

The question throbbed in her brain. Who had survived, and for how long?

Soon the whole world would know the answer.

Including, unfortunately, the client.

## MILAN

# FLOATING

MILAN STARTED FOLLOWING THE STREAM AGAIN, BUT IT WAS hard going. Every step she took she sank six inches deep in the soft snow. Lifting each boot high, and then punching it down again, was exhausting. Her steps grew slower and shorter.

Milan had been snowshoeing once before, on rental snowshoes. The snow had been like this, soft and deep and almost impossible to walk in. But once she'd buckled on the snowshoes, walking had felt like floating.

Old-fashioned snowshoes were made from interlaced canes that distributed the wearer's weight over a larger surface area. All around her were evergreens. If she strapped branches to her feet, could they do the same thing?

But strapped with what? The pilot's shoelaces were already being used to tow the sled. She unzipped the duffel bag. One of his T-shirts was lighter, made of cotton. Maybe she could tear it into strips. Using her teeth, Milan tried to bite a hole in it. She only succeeded in frustrating herself.

Then she remembered the nail scissors in the dopp kit. She stripped the sock from her right hand. It was hard to press the tiny metal handles with her numb fingers, but finally she made a hole in the cloth a few inches above the hem. By cutting and pulling she eventually had a strip of cloth about an inch and a half wide. She repeated the process to make a second strip.

Now she needed two branches. Wary of falling into another tree well, Milan stayed well away from the trunk when she approached a nearby evergreen. After some twisting and bending, she managed to snap off two similar-sized branches. Each was about three feet long and a foot and a half wide, with clusters of green twigs on either side.

She laid them on the ground parallel to each other, the widest parts facing forward. The branches curved on the ends. She flipped one so both curves went up. After stepping on them, she tied the branches to the front part of her boots with the torn T-shirt strips.

Milan picked up the remaining golf club and took a few experimental steps. Even though she still had to raise her feet so the branches didn't catch when she walked, the going was much easier. And when she turned around after a dozen steps, her tracks were half-erased, not the easy-to-follow series of holes her boots had left. If someone really was hunting her, they would have a harder time following her trail.

Ms. Robbins had told her she was smart, and right now Milan felt like it might be true. She began walking next to the stream, thinking about how proud her parents would be of her. If her mom were here, she would praise Milan for never giving up. Her mom's favorite quote was from Amelia Earhart: "The most difficult thing is the decision to act. The rest is merely tenacity."

And her dad had taught her how powerful it was to shift your focus on a long hike. Instead of talking about how far you'd walked, you should think about the interesting finds you'd spotted. Instead of constantly asking how much farther, you should think about how yummy your lunch would be.

Lunch. Milan's stomach rumbled. She would kill for even a granola bar. She imagined biting into a toasted cheese sandwich. Sucking her fingers after eating hot fries dusted with salt. Sinking her fork into the first velvety bite of German chocolate cake, with pecans and coconut, the kind her mom always made for her birthday. Tears sparked her eyes. She would never hike with her dad again. She would never taste her mom's cake, or watch *The Wizard of Oz* with her, the way they did every year. If she could have them back, she would never argue, never talk back.

What good was appreciating what you had lost if it was still gone forever?

The sun was fully over the horizon now. Milan turned to look back. The white-peaked mountain where they had crashed looked like a picture you'd see printed on a box of instant cocoa. From here, there wasn't even a single black speck marring the perfect, benign surface. She turned around.

Thirty minutes later, Milan heard a *whup-whup-whup* overhead. She tilted her head back and squinted.

A helicopter.

# Chapter 32

## MILAN
## TOO TIRED TO SCREAM

THE HELICOPTER WAS PASSING OVERHEAD, FLYING TOWARD THE scene of the crash. Should Milan wave her arms, try to get into a clearing?

But her body made the decision for her even as her mind was asking the question. Instead of trying to attract attention, Milan shoved her way into some low bushes bordering the stream. With luck, they wouldn't provide as much contrast to her black parka as the snow did. She tilted her head down so the pale oval of her face didn't betray her. She imagined the men on board the helicopter scanning the ground with high-powered binoculars.

*Don't trust anyone.* Her mom's words echoed in her head. An idea that might have seemed like a head injury–induced delusion if Milan hadn't seen the drone hovering over her body.

Whoever had killed both her parents would clearly stop at nothing to keep their secrets hidden. And right now the literal key to those secrets was next to Milan's heart. Maybe the people on the helicopter were trustworthy, but what about all the people who would come if they reported finding her? All it would take would be one stranger claiming they were there to help her when really they planned to finish the job.

As she listened to the *whup-whup* fade away, Milan tried to calm her racing heart. How many times could her body startle before it shut down altogether? A wave of weariness swept over her. She had to brace her hands on her knees to keep from tumbling to the ground.

Only when the sky was silent did Milan push her way back out of the undergrowth. After retying one of her homemade snowshoes, she set out again.

She walked. She walked. She walked. Her head pounded with each step. White dots swarmed her field of vision and then faded away. She drank more water from the stream, making sure to let it warm in her mouth before she swallowed. Occasionally she sang to herself, sometimes "Amazing Grace," sometimes bits of "Don't Stop Believin'," a song both her parents had thought was corny but still loved to sing along to.

It was just before noon—Milan wouldn't allow herself

to think of it as lunchtime—when she spotted a puzzling heap under a tree. It was partly covered by snow, pieces of bark, and broken branches. Whatever it was, it was big. Nearly as big as her. As she got closer, she saw brownish-gray fur interspersed with patches of bright red and pearlescent white. Every step revealed a new nightmarish detail. Dark, sightless eyes. A long snout that ended in a black nose. A pinkish-gray lolling tongue that would never be pulled back into a broken jaw.

It was a deer. A half-eaten deer. Its blood spattered all over the snow.

Milan was too tired to scream, but her mind screamed for her. And before she could even begin to think about what had killed it, eaten half of it, and then hidden it, there was a growl behind her.

# Chapter 33

## JANIE
# BEAR THINKING ABOUT

**Two and a half years earlier**

ALL AROUND JANIE, FARMLAND WAS GETTING RIPPED UP LIKE OLD material for a patchwork quilt. Five gas wells had already been drilled around her farm. Less than a mile away was an injection well where they squirted the fracked water back deep into the ground.

Early on, most of her neighbors just took the money from the gas leases and sold their herds. Before, there had been a dozen dairy farmers around her. Now only three were still running. But dairy farming was in Janie's blood.

Of her 146 acres, Prospect Power ended up using 22 for development: a well pad that held all the equipment, plus space for access roads and pipelines. Unfortunately, the most suitable site for the well pad turned out to be only a few hundred feet from the house.

Janie should have realized nothing in life was free. Reality was a little different from how Steve had painted it. It was like reading a book about Niagara Falls versus standing under it in a shower cap.

The lights of the rig shone day and night into the house, which vibrated with the constant thrum of the generators, punctuated by horns and backup beepers. Out on their rural road, ten to fifteen semis regularly sat idling. One knocked down her mailbox, although no one would ever own up to it.

On some days, the sky turned brown. Wrinkling her nose, Noelle complained about the near-constant unidentifiable smell that could only be described as a stink. Worst of all was the water, both in the well and in the creek that cut through their land. Fracking was water and sand and just a few chemicals, according to Steve. But which ones? Because the water that had once run gin-clear was now murky.

Town was starting to change, too. The radio said crime had gone up by about 30 percent. Rents were skyrocketing, and many of the locals couldn't afford to eat at the restaurant where Becca worked anymore, not after they raised the prices.

Janie developed a rash. So did many of her cows. What about their milk? It didn't bear thinking about.

# Chapter 34

# MILAN

## PREY

AT THE SOUND OF THE LONG GROWL BEHIND HER, MILAN RESISTED the urge to whirl around. Instead she moved slowly and deliberately. Even though she had half guessed what it was, when she saw the mountain lion twenty feet away, the blood in her veins turned to ice.

It was long and lean, tawny brown with a lighter face and chest. Panic fluttered in Milan's throat as she took in its powerful shoulders, its thick front legs that ended in paws far bigger than her own hands. The gray claws, outlined by black fur, were as thick as talons.

It bared its fangs to reveal the pink, wet flesh of its tongue. Its long tail was held low, the black tip twitching slightly. Milan had seen enough cats stalking birds to recognize that posture. It was hunting her. She shivered, feeling like a cold finger was tracing her spine.

"Go away," she said. She meant to shout, but it came out as a hoarse whisper. Her legs were shaking.

Staring at her with yellow eyes, the mountain lion responded with a chirping growl that was half question, half answer, as if debating with itself what to do. Its fangs were at least two inches long and wickedly sharp. A thread of saliva connected the upper and lower canines.

If it could take down a full-size deer, how much challenge did one girl pose? Milan had no hooves. No horns. No long legs to bound away on. She had just two feet to its four. If she turned and made a run for it, it would be on her in seconds. Hot breath on the back of her neck, and then the fangs sinking into her spinal cord.

The mountain lion took one step forward, then another, moving with sinuous grace, hips at an angle so that it looked skewed.

Never breaking eye contact, Milan slowly backed away from both the cat and the cache. She tugged the sled after her with each step, fighting the urge to turn and run. Running was what prey did. Surely, that was what the deer had done, the deer that was now nothing but blood and bones and shredded fur.

Eyes never leaving hers, the mountain lion took a step toward her, and then another.

"No!" Milan said, her voice louder, and stamped her foot.

In response, the mountain lion laid its tattered ears back. But it didn't stop coming. Still, even though it was matching her step for step, the distance between them had stopped narrowing. The sled—moving, but clearly not alive—might be making it nervous.

Milan kept shuffling backward, away from the cache. Maybe she could make it decide what it wanted more. Her or the deer it already had.

With her peripheral vision, she scanned the area. If she broke the staring contest, the mountain lion might see her as weaker. About twenty feet away was a leafless tree. The branches started just five feet above the ground. But even if she could somehow manage to climb up into it before the mountain lion clawed the backs of her thighs, she was pretty sure it could climb a tree just as well as a cat.

The pilot's gun was in the duffel bag. But by the time Milan unzipped the bag, found the gun, and figured out if it had a safety or anything, it would be far too late.

What could she do? If she tried to hide, to crouch, the mountain lion would see her as small. And it needed to see her as big. It needed to see her as too much of a challenge to be worth it. How could she make herself look less appealing? More predator than prey? In an attempt to look bigger, Milan raised her arms. Only then did she remember the golf club.

Swinging it back and forth over her head, she stamped her feet and bellowed. "Leave me alone! Leave me alone!"

The mountain lion paused, one paw still raised. It seemed to be considering her. Its tongue slicked out.

A movement in the corner of her eye made Milan turn her head slightly. The mountain lion was now on her right. How was that possible? Milan's eyes flicked back and forth. There were two. Two! But the first one was bigger. Then she understood. A mother and her nearly full-grown offspring. How many kills did it take to feed two mountain lions? How hard had it been this winter to keep them both fed? Both cats looked lean. Too lean? How hungry were they?

"No," Milan shouted again, waving the golf club even more vigorously. "No, Momma, leave me alone. Or I'll hurt your baby."

The mother mountain lion stayed back. But like any teenager, the younger mountain lion was more willing to take risks. Willing to make mistakes.

Ears laid back, it rushed at her, powerful back legs like springs pushing it forward. As it leaped, it spread its front legs to each side, oddly reminiscent of someone opening their arms for a hug. But no one had ever tried to hug Milan with slitted eyes and a wide-open mouth filled with teeth as sharp as knives.

It landed less than ten feet away. Had it pulled up short? Misjudged the distance? Maybe it was just trying to intimidate her into freezing, the way a cornered rabbit might. Whatever the reason, it gathered itself for another leap, one that would definitely get to her.

Milan screamed, shuffling backward faster and more frantically. But she forgot to lift her feet. One of the branches strapped to her boots caught in the snow, and suddenly she was off-balance. She was falling.

*No!*

Time stretched out like taffy.

In her mind's eye, Milan saw her inevitable future. Once she was on the ground, both mountain lions would go for her. Her thick parka wouldn't save her vulnerable face or the back of her neck. They'd claw her until she was blind, bite her spinal cord until she couldn't move.

And even as she saw her future, Milan stabbed behind her with the golf club, took a giant step backward, and somehow managed to stay on her feet.

"No! Leave me alone!" she shouted. The yell scraped out of her throat, so loud it hurt her own ears.

But while the mother lion retreated with a hiss, the younger one leaped at her again, front legs moving in and out in that weird half-hug motion.

With another scream, Milan grabbed the head of the golf club with both hands and then swung it with all her might. The handle struck the cat's left shoulder so hard it had to scramble to stay on its feet. The shock of the impact traveled all the way up Milan's body. With a squeal, the younger mountain lion retreated.

Its mother hissed again, ears laid flat to her head. But when she moved, it was not forward, but sideways, closer to the younger mountain lion. She was ready to defend her cub.

The younger one was caught between desire and fear. But when Milan raised the golf club again, it flinched away.

The older mountain lion let out a bloodcurdling wail. Milan recognized it as the sound that had haunted her dreams. Not a woman screaming. But a mountain lion.

This was their territory, not hers, and they were only doing what they needed to do to live. Same as her.

But Milan refused to be prey.

# Chapter 35

# MILAN
## THROUGH HER VEINS

MILAN KEPT WALKING BACKWARD, LIFTING HER FEET HIGH TO keep her makeshift snowshoes from catching. She didn't turn around even when the two mountain lions did, trotting back in the direction of the cached deer.

What if it was a ruse? Milan couldn't catch her breath. What if one of the big cats circled back and started slinking right next to her, hidden by trees and bushes, a shadow she never caught sight of until it was too late?

The idea filled her head like a balloon, pressing out all other thoughts. Adrenaline coursed through her in waves, buzzing through her veins one moment and leaving her spent the next.

In her mad panic to get away, Milan hadn't paid attention

to what direction she was going. Where was the stream? Her chest was tight, her heart was racing. Panicked, she tried to recognize something, anything. She needed the stream to eventually lead her out of the wilderness. But the mountain lions needed it, too, for drinking water. She would just have to hope she was heading in the same general direction as downstream.

Only what direction was that? Milan turned in a slow circle, the snow making soft noises underfoot. The trees stared blankly back. Everything looked the same and nothing looked familiar. Even if she wanted to, she couldn't retrace her own steps. The marks the branches turned snowshoes left were too faint to be easily visible. Her head was on a swivel and her breath wouldn't stop shaking.

She touched the tattoo on her wrist through the layers of socks. What would her dad do? Her brain felt sludgy. Did it need calories to work? She hadn't eaten, had barely slept, and had already demanded far too much from her body. She couldn't fix any of those things, but her dad was always talking about the importance of hydration.

After drinking from her 3-1-1 bag again, Milan felt her shoulders straighten, like a drooping plant that had just been watered.

She stuffed more snow in the bag, tucked it back into place without examining her broken finger, and scanned the horizon. There. A certain fold of hills seemed familiar. She set off.

As she walked, she kept catching her makeshift snow-shoes. The surface here was getting harder. Firmer. The snow that had fallen around her overnight hadn't reached this far. Finally she untied the bindings and stuffed them in her pocket, then walked forward on her own two feet, leaving the branches behind.

A bird flew overhead, black wings against a blue sky. Milan tracked it with her eyes for a moment, then dropped her gaze back down to the white snow, the emerald ever-greens. But no dark line of a stream. At least not yet.

Her dad's one passion had always been this—the cli-mate, the earth, the pristine wilderness. It was why he had become a senator: So that he might have the power to change things. He had done it for Milan, and for the mil-lions of future children who would suffer if the world kept getting warmer and drier and more inhospitable, with ris-ing oceans and storms that kept breaking records set only the year before.

Of course, even her dad hadn't been perfect. He'd owned a private plane. But right before he died, he'd put a deposit down on one of the electric ones that would soon be on the market.

Thinking of the plane made Milan think of the bomb. What had her dad found out that had been enough to get both him and her mom killed? And this was clearly more than just someone with a grudge. According to her mom, all these deaths had been the result of a conspiracy.

For the past few months, Milan had hated her mom for ripping her away from everything she'd known after she had already lost her dad. But now she saw things with new eyes. Worried she herself might be a target, her mom had needed to keep them apart. She had been trying to keep Milan safe.

"I'm sorry, Mom," Milan said out loud, breaking the stillness. But then she heard another sound. A soft burbling. A few feet later, she saw it. The stream, wider now.

"Thank you," she said, again to empty air. Was she talking to her parents, to God, to Nature herself? All she knew was she didn't feel as alone.

Through sheer force of will, she kept walking, kept moving. She was exhausted, depleted, her legs like cooked spaghetti.

She sang wordless snatches of old Beatles songs. She prayed. She talked to her dead parents. They felt very close, as if they were hovering over her, looking down. Her dad would tell her to keep calm. Her mom would tell her to keep going. They would tell her she was smart. Smarter than this situation. Smart enough to get out of here and find the one man who would know how to help her. Mr. Kirkby.

But first she had to get out of these endless woods. She was racing death. It would be easy to let death win. She was moving more and more slowly. Getting mad at herself, Milan slapped her cheek with a socked hand. It didn't sting nearly enough. After pulling the sock off with her teeth, she repeated the slap, only harder. "You need to suck it up, Milan. If you quit, you die. No one's going to hand you a blanket and a cup of cocoa." Not here, not now.

Not ever again.

Part of her thought she should just lie down. Give up. Let death come. But then her mom's voice rang out in her head. "Are you kidding me? If you lie down, then we will have died for nothing."

"Keep going," she heard her dad say. "Do not stop. You have to move. Movement is life."

The stream was getting wider. When Milan had first found it, she could have stepped across it. Now it was at least ten feet wide. A big chunk of the afternoon had already gone by.

Milan checked her phone, as she already had done dozens of times. But this time, something was different. For a second, it showed a single bar of service. Even as she gasped, it blinked out.

But soon that bar would stay.

And then what should she do?

# Chapter 36

## MILAN
## PULL THE TRIGGER

EVEN KNOWING IT WAS EVENTUALLY GOING TO HAPPEN, IT STILL felt like a hallucination or a dream when Milan saw a single, steady bar on her phone.

She halted, staring at the tiny rectangle. Now what?

Her first instinct was to call 911. But just like flagging down the helicopter, calling 911 would trigger a maelstrom. The whole world would soon learn she'd survived. But her mom had insisted everyone had to keep believing she was dead.

The first step was figuring out where she was. She clicked on Google Maps. It took a long time to load.

While it did, she thought. The bodies inside the plane must have been reduced to little more than ash. It would take investigators time to figure out that she and Eric were missing. Maybe they never would.

But the fact that her mom's body would be found outside the plane would raise questions, especially if they realized someone else had survived. Whoever brought down the plane would want to know if her mom had said anything. Milan touched the outline of the key ring in her front coat pocket.

Google Maps had finally loaded. Milan zoomed and clicked, trying to figure out where she was in relationship to everything else. If she continued to follow the stream, in about three miles she would come to a road. On city streets, she could walk three miles in fifty minutes, easy. Given her exhaustion and the snowy terrain, it would certainly take longer.

After that, she would need to find a ride to Bend, the nearest large town. From there she could figure out a way to get to Portland.

Should she call Mr. Kirkby and ask him to come rescue her? But she didn't have his phone number and didn't know how to get through to him without admitting who she was.

No, it was better to go to Mr. Kirkby's house. She'd been there many times with her parents, for dinner or parties when she was too young to stay at home by herself. She would watch movies in one of his guest rooms and eventually fall asleep.

Milan had already done the impossible. She had survived a plane crash, falling in a tree well, and a mountain lion attack. She could figure out how to retrieve the information her parents had died for and then how to get to Mr. Kirkby with no one being the wiser.

But what about Eric? Milan might be the only living person who knew he was actually alive. But once the bad guys discovered the truth, Milan and Eric would both be loose ends needing to be tied up. Would Eric know enough to put the dots together when he heard about the plane crash? Would he realize he needed to lie low, to hide, to find someone who could keep him safe?

Eric had always had time for Milan, sometimes when her own parents hadn't. Some of her earliest memories were of playing Connect Four and Go Fish with him, playing for Goldfish or pennies. And those friendly wagers of his—he would bet a dollar on nearly anything. How long Milan could hold her breath, how many books she could read in a week, how many french fries would be in a box. Occasionally, he had bet a dollar she couldn't be quiet for fifteen minutes, a genius move Milan had stolen once she started babysitting. He had a scar on his calf from when they'd been racing bikes and she'd accidentally turned into him. He'd never ratted her out, claiming he had run into a curb after borrowing her bike.

She composed a text to Eric. **Bomb blew up our plane. Everyone else dead. Be careful. Don't tell anyone I'm alive.**

After she hit the Send key, Milan stared at her phone. Whoever had blown up her mom's plane, flipped her dad's car—was anything too hard for them? Could they track her phone?

With trembling fingers, she powered it off, praying she hadn't just signed both her and Eric's death warrants.

Milan kept going, staggering as much as walking. Earlier she had been hungry, but now she felt past all physical desires, like a machine that had been set into motion and would keep going until the batteries gave out. Her feet were wooden pegs.

Once she reached the road, she would flag down a ride. She would need a cover story that didn't involve plane crashes or climbing down a mountain. Could she say she had gone hiking alone and gotten lost?

But why mention the mountain at all? Maybe she could say she had argued with her boyfriend and gotten out of the car. But a girl turning up near where a girl might have disappeared—it wouldn't be hard to put the pieces together later.

Plus, people thought girls were vulnerable. Weak. A girl on her own might make an adult decide they had to take care of her—or take advantage of her.

But what if she wasn't a girl? Milan's voice was deep enough that more than one caller to their Portland landline had thought she was her dad. She was five foot nine, tall for a girl, and wearing man's pants. All these layers would obscure her size. If Milan kept her hood up, could she pass as a guy? Try to sound and act like Chance?

Even dirty and scratched, her fine-boned hands might give her away. She would have to keep them hidden. Plus the broken finger would raise questions.

To be a dude, she would also need a new name.

When she was about seven, her dad had patiently listened to Milan's long-winded and completely unconvincing lie about what had happened to some leftover cake, a lie that involved an open window and the neighbor's cat. Now she heard his voice in her head again. *The best way to tell a lie is to keep it as close to the truth as possible.* Then he'd paused. *Don't ever tell your mom I told you that.*

So her new name needed to sound enough like her real one so that Milan would turn her head if she heard it. But was there a guy's name that sounded enough like hers? Milan started making her way through the alphabet, mouthing potential variants. Allen. Was anyone named Calen?

Dylan was pretty good but it stressed the first syllable instead of the second, the way Milan did. Dion was closer, but lacked the "L" sound that might help catch her attention.

Then she came to the letter *L*. Leon. She said it out loud, and then her own name. Leon. Milan. Pretty close.

The sound of an engine in front of her made her head jerk up. From the sound of it, the road was only a few feet away. She fought the urge to run. Before she tried to get a ride, she needed to get rid of the golf club and the sled. There was no possible cover story where she had a golf club and a piece of an aircraft.

But she would keep the gun. If things got bad, Milan could point it at someone.

They didn't need to know she had no idea how to use it and would be too afraid to pull the trigger.

# Chapter 37

# LENNY
# SALVAGE

ALL MORNING, LENNY HAD ALTERNATED BETWEEN CHECKING HER laptop and pacing around the hotel room. She was like the bear at a roadside zoo she'd visited when she was eleven. Karl had driven them to the coast for a rare vacation. After passing billboard after billboard commanding PET THE CUB NOW! he had finally given in to Lenny's nagging.

But once he paid their admission fee and they walked in, even an eleven-year-old could see how depressing the whole setup was. A sign affixed to the bars of the chimp's cage warned that it liked to throw its feces. The tiger lay in the corner, ignoring the people who hissed at it and rattled the wire enclosure. The promised cub was a sickly looking leopard cub that stayed limp as it was passed from hand to hand. Ten dollars got you a photo of your grinning face pressed next to its whiskers.

But it was the bear that had really gotten to Lenny. Chained by the neck to a metal pole, the brown bear never stopped walking the whole time they were there. It had already worn a three-inch-deep dusty circle in the grass, circling endlessly around the pole. She and her father had looked at each other. Lenny was horrified. An outsider would have said Karl's expression was neutral, but she saw the slight narrowing in his eyes.

Late that night, when the so-called zoo was closed, they returned. After spray-painting the security cameras, Karl had Lenny pick the lock. The Master padlock opened after only a few rakes of her pick. When they walked through the gate, the animals stared dully at them.

And then Karl had put his hand on Lenny's shoulder and handed her his gun, and she had shot the bear through the heart. He had taken care of the others.

Now Lenny pushed the memory aside and sat back down at her laptop. From hacking into all the applicable systems, she knew the recovery mission had made it to the scene of the crash site. Heather was definitely dead. The itemized list of everything that had been found on her body included nothing of interest to Lenny. Inside the plane, remains had been recovered, charred beyond all recognition. So far, no one seemed to know the plane crash had been anything but a tragic accident.

While there had as yet been no formal announcement of Heather's death, word was spreading. With social media, you didn't even need to be a hacker. People were happy to put their life online—Instagramming their meals, Facebooking their event plans, tweeting their locations and opinions.

Heather's Facebook feed was flooded with condolences, expressions of disbelief, and praying hand emojis. Her name was trending on Twitter. Her picture had been posted to the website of a national news network.

Sometimes Lenny wished she had been born in the same era as Karl. Before the age of social media, facial recognition software, video surveillance, and biometric identification. While she used those tools for her job, did they really make life any better?

Her laptop chimed. Someone was using Milan's phone. Lenny's pulse sped up. Whoever had it was checking Google Maps. Which meant as soon as they located themselves, Lenny did, too. Despite how impossible it was, they had managed to make it down the mountain.

So who had Milan's phone? Someone smart enough to realize their own phone might be watched. Who didn't realize Lenny had trackers on all of them. It was the things you ignored that came back to bite you.

After opening a second window on her laptop, Lenny put in the geo coordinates. The survivor was about three miles from a road. And that road was about forty minutes from Bend.

Okay, okay. She could handle this. She should be able to get to them before they got to the road.

But then it got worse. Because they sent a text. To Eric! **Bomb blew up our plane. Everyone else dead. Be careful. Don't tell anyone I'm alive.**

Eric wasn't dead? How could that be? The swear words crowded into Lenny's head and she let her lips silently shape them. Where was Eric? What did he know? And what was he going to do with that knowledge?

She had to put a stop to all of it. Her first priority was to find the phone and take care of its current owner.

As her thoughts raced, whoever currently had the phone powered it off. It disappeared from her screen. Smart.

Too smart.

Paranoid now, Lenny checked everyone's phones. Eric's hadn't been used since yesterday. But its last location was not aboard the plane, but at the DC private jet terminal. Why hadn't he boarded?

Lenny always liked to have the upper hand, but now she was on the back foot.

It felt like she was losing her edge. What if the client felt the same?

She had to salvage this job.

Fast.

# Chapter 38

## MILAN
# LAST HOUSE ON THE LEFT

WHEN MILAN STEPPED OUT ONTO THE ROAD, SHE WANTED TO FALL down and kiss the cracked tarmac. Visions of flushing toilets and hot showers and steaming plates of food filled her head.

The minutes crawled by as Milan waited for a car to approach. Mindlessly, she kept humming the same six or seven notes. When it became clear it might be a while, she started walking, rehearsing her cover story. Her name was Leon. Her—*his*—car had broken down on a logging road and *he* had hiked out.

Would anyone really stop? Everyone knew hitchhikers were either serial killers or soon to be victims of a serial killer. But she couldn't walk to Bend. She could barely walk another step.

When she finally heard an engine, her body spent a bit more of its adrenaline as she startled and then whirled around. She stuck out her right hand, then realized that with a sock over it there was no digit to provide the universal gesture. Grabbing the end in her teeth, she pulled it off just in time to stick out her thumb.

It was a tan sedan, driven by a woman with blond hair. She stared at Milan and kept staring as she passed without even slowing down.

Milan's shoulders sagged and she turned back around. But only a minute later she again heard the sound of an engine.

This time it was an old blue-and-white truck driven by a small man with red cheeks and close-cropped white hair. He stopped next to Milan, leaned over, and manually rolled down the passenger-side window halfway.

"Where do you need a ride to, son?"

Milan closed her eyes for a second and let out a breath. "Bend," she said in as low a voice as she could muster. "My car broke down on an old logging road." She vaguely waved her hand. "If I can get into town, I have a friend who can come back with me and tow me out."

*Too much detail*, her brain screamed.

"You can put your bag in the truck bed," the old man said.

Only after Milan put down the pilot's duffel did she remember the gun. This guy looked the opposite of threatening, but looks could be deceiving. Still, there was no easy way to retrieve it, so she just got in.

After she closed the door, the old man's nostrils flared. In the small, enclosed space, even Milan could smell herself. Sweat from exertion and panic and bone-deep exhaustion had wet and then dried a million times on her underarms, her feet, and the small of her back.

Maybe her body odor would help convince this man that she was male. Or it might make him kick her out. But he didn't say anything, just drove.

Automatically, she reached over her shoulder for the seat belt. Her sock-covered fingers found nothing. Realizing her right hand was still bare, she tucked it under her thigh, hoping he hadn't paid it any attention.

"Lap belt only, I'm afraid," the man said. "My name's Harold."

"Leon."

He nodded. "Leon. I know that means *lion* in Greek."

Milan acted like this was old news. The thought was oddly comforting.

"When my wife was still alive, we were trying to learn Greek so we could understand the New Testament better."

"I'm sorry that she's gone," Milan said. Her own mourning for her parents colored the sentence.

"She just got to heaven a little sooner than me," Harold

said. "She always liked to be early to things." He pointed at an old-fashioned flip phone lying on the dash. "Want to use my phone to call your friend?"

Should Milan pretend to call someone? But what if Harold looked at his call log later? That would only raise more questions.

"I already talked to him," she improvised. "He was at work. He said he wouldn't be able to come get my car until tomorrow." She was making it up as she went along. Why hadn't she thought this through more?

It would take about an hour to drive to Bend. Harold didn't ask a single question about Milan's flimsy story. He just listened to an oldies station, which faded in and out, tapping his fingers on the steering wheel. Even when the interior of the truck grew too warm for how she was dressed, Milan kept her hood pulled low and her coat zipped up to her neck. Feeling weak, almost boneless, she leaned her head against the cold of the window and closed her eyes.

When she woke up, they were just passing a sign saying they were entering the city. A block later, Harold said, "I need to get gas," and pulled into a Chevron station. Across the highway was a strip mall and a run-down motel with a sign reading STAY-A-WHILE MOTEL. WI-FI. IN-ROOM COFFEE.

"I'll just get out here." Milan reached for the door handle. "Thanks for the ride."

Harold cleared his throat. "Are you sure you're going

to be okay, Leon? I can take you wherever you need to go. Or maybe treat you to a meal? You look like you could use some food."

Her throat clogged with tears even as her stomach rumbled. "No, this is fine. My friend doesn't live too far from here."

Harold tilted his head and regarded her. "If you change your mind, I just live a few blocks from here on China-berry. Last house on the left. White with blue shutters."

"Thanks," Milan said, trying to make her voice as gruff and rough as Chance's could be. She forced herself to open the door. "But I'll be okay."

"I won't keep you, then," Harold said.

Milan got out, closed the door, and gave him a little wave through the window. After shouldering the pilot's duffel, she set off as if she had someplace to go.

It was hard to walk away from what felt like safety. What felt like protection. When you had parents, you had a guarantee that no matter what you did, someone would always love you. Someone would be willing to sacrifice everything for you.

Milan had never felt more alone.

# Chapter 39

JANIE

# TO BE EXPECTED

**Two and a half years earlier**

"I NEED TO SPEAK TO STEVE HAMILL," JANIE TOLD THE RECEPTION-
ist at Prospect Power. Janie was wearing the nice pantsuit
she normally reserved for church.

The girl, who was younger than Becca, looked her up
and down. "Do you have an appointment?"

Janie did not have an appointment. How many messages had she left Steve that he hadn't returned? It was just
as frustrating as talking to the EPA, the DEQ, or any other
three-letter acronym agency she had tried to call. The gov-
ernment folks would listen to her rattle on and then do
nothing.

Past the girl's shoulder was a door with a nameplate

on it. Engraved with Steve's name. Without answering, she walked past the girl and opened the door.

Steve was on the phone. His eyes went wide when he saw Janie and he took his feet off his desk. "Sorry, Ed— something just came up. I'm going to have to call you back," he said, and then hung up. "Janie? To what do I owe the pleasure?"

The receptionist hurried in. "I'm sorry, Mr. Hamill, she just busted right past me!"

He held up his hand. "That's okay, Virginia. Sometimes we all forget the protocols."

"The protocols. Right." She nodded furiously. "I'm sorry." She left the room.

Guessing she didn't have much time, Janie took the glass Mason jar from her purse and held it out. "I trusted you when you told me your stories about your grandkids and your dog. You said we would hardly notice. Well, this is my well water now." It was murky, tinted a milky brown. It looked like the bathwater after one of the kids had been playing in the mud. "You've been telling me my water would be safe to drink."

"And it is. A little sedimentation is to be expected, at least at first."

She unscrewed the lid and set the jar on his desk with a thump. The water sloshed, splashing onto the polished wood. "Okay, you drink it, then."

Steve regarded it and then looked back up at her. "I'm not thirsty." He set his mouth.

"Our water was good before you started drilling," Janie said as two burly security guards came into the room. "And now there's something wrong with our cows."

Janie had few rules, but they were rock-solid. If you made a mess, you cleaned it up. If you hurt people, you made it right.

And if someone did you wrong, you didn't smile and take it.

# Chapter 40

## MILAN

# HER LAST MEAL

MILAN PRESSED THE BUTTON FOR THE CROSSWALK. AS SHE WAITED for the light to turn, a wave of weakness passed over her. She put a hand on the pole to steady herself. Which to do first: eat or sleep? The yellow-and-red Denny's sign beckoned. She was exhausted, but she needed food even more. She crossed the street, pulled open the door, and walked in. The smell of food made her mouth flood.

The waitress was dressed from head to toe in black, except for a big yellow name tag pinned to her chest. It said ANGEL. Her brown hair was slicked back into a tight ponytail.

When Angel looked at her, her lip curled like Milan was homeless. She guessed she was now. Without your family, a home was just a house.

After picking up a menu, Angel gestured for Milan to follow her. The table she took her to was in the back, well away from the other three tables that were occupied. She handed her a menu and then left.

Milan sat down, setting the duffel by her feet. The last time she had been at a Denny's was with Chance after a concert. She wished he was here with her, with his dark eyes and his mouth that always gave away his feelings before he thought to straighten out his lips. She amended her wish. She wished she was back in that time and place, laughing, talking, slapping his hand when he tried to steal fries from her plate. With her parents still alive to give her a lecture if she came home late.

As she turned the menu's heavy laminated pages and looked at the photos of mostly tan food, her stomach spasmed. Her hunger was so big it bordered on nausea.

Angel returned, pulling an order pad out of her short black apron. Her tired eyes were lined all the way around. Milan was glad she hadn't bothered to put on makeup yesterday—was it only yesterday? She didn't have to worry that traces of eyeshadow or liner would give her away.

Trying to keep her voice low and rough, she said, "I'll have the Loaded Veggie Omelette. And a side of pancakes. Oh, and a chocolate milkshake."

Angel's pen paused. "So you want me to sub out the toast for pancakes?"

"No. I want both. Whole wheat toast, please. And water. Lots of water."

Angel tilted her head. "I'm afraid I'm going to have to ask you to prepay."

Milan didn't even bother arguing. She just reached into the inside chest pocket of her coat and pulled out the first bill she touched. It was a fifty. "This should be more than enough."

Angel nodded, but the crisp bill actually seemed to make her more suspicious. "I'll be back soon with your order. And your water."

Milan glanced around to see if anyone else was looking at her. No one was. She had become the kind of person other people would rather not see. Angel came back with two red plastic cups filled with water. Milan downed one in a long, single gulp. Maybe she should go to the bathroom, more to assess the damage than to pee. But when she looked toward the back, the restaurant had gendered bathrooms. Picking a side might draw too much attention.

Her hands, though. Her left still had a sock pulled over it, but her right was scratched, bruised, and dirty, with torn nails. She took a napkin from the dispenser and dipped it in the remaining cup of water. She used it and then a second one to wipe the worst of the dirt off her fingers and palm.

Next Milan slipped out the rest of the money she had

taken from her mom and counted it underneath the table. Three hundred seventy dollars. More than enough for a meal, a room, and a bus ride to Portland. Not nearly enough to stay hidden forever. Maybe she could find a room on Craigslist, find a job that paid under the table. Take a new name and identity and hope her parents' killers never realized the truth.

But that's not what her mom had asked her to do. And after she gave her parents' secrets to Mr. Kirkby, he'd take charge. Maybe fulfill his role of godfather by having her move in with him. Although he'd always been a little awkward around her—he didn't have children of his own—so maybe she'd just end up in another boarding school.

Thinking about the future was exhausting. Focus on the now, Milan told herself.

The pancakes came out first. She doused them with the entire miniature carafe of fake syrup. The first bite was cloying and delicious, like eating a thin, sticky, sweet sponge. She shoved in another bite and then a third. The pancakes practically dissolved in her mouth. She drank the last of the second glass of water to wash them down.

Angel came back out with the milkshake and the omelette, complete with hash browns and whole wheat toast glistening with butter. After seeing Milan's two empty water glasses, she returned with a pitcher and filled them up.

Milan was eating more slowly, her thoughts thick as

mud. The crisp shards of fried grated potatoes snapped between her teeth like tiny french fries. She alternated bites of toast, omelette, and hash browns with long pulls on the milkshake. Her stomach was a round ball pressing against all her layers, but she still ate as if it might be her last meal.

Finally, Milan leaned against the wall and closed her eyes. The sounds of the other customers, the scrape of their forks and knives on the plates, the low murmur of conversation, were soothing.

She knew it wasn't true, but she finally felt safe.

# Chapter 41

LENNY
# TO HAVE A FAMILY

ALTHOUGH IT WASN'T CURRENTLY SNOWING, LENNY PULLED UP her coat hood and ducked her head when she left her room. The sprawling hotel had few security cameras. These days, though, everyone had a camera in their pocket.

Her phone was set to alert her if or when whoever was using Milan's phone came back online. But it wasn't hard to figure out what the phone's current owner would do. Take the shortest path to the nearest road and get out of there. All Lenny had to do was beat them there.

As she turned out of the parking lot fast enough for the Subaru's tires to squeal, her thoughts returned to what the survivor had done with the phone. Or what they hadn't done. They had turned off the phone and they hadn't called 911. That meant they guessed or even knew it might be safer if they were off the grid, out of official hands.

Lenny turned onto the highway. Not calling 911 was just more proof that whoever had Milan's phone now was not its original owner.

In all the months she had surveilled the family, she had come to like Milan. Sometimes she would even turn on the girl's phone camera just to catch a glimpse of her. Milan and that neighbor boy, Chance Diaz, had shared a mutual crush, even if neither of them seemed to have realized it. Milan was a smart, spirited girl. She took in everything and filed it away for future reference. Just like her mother, who wouldn't stop tugging on the threads of her husband's death. And, just like her mother, Milan had been in the wrong place at the wrong time. It wasn't his family's fault that Jack Mayhew had attracted the attention of Lenny's client.

Had Lenny made a mistake, putting all her eggs in one basket? It had been at least a year since she had worked for anyone else. What had seemed like a mutually beneficial relationship was putting her at risk. She knew a lot about the client. Probably too much.

Following the GPS, she left the highway for a smaller road. Narrow and twisting, it didn't even have shoulders, just the occasional passing lane. The Subaru was no sports car, but Lenny pushed it to its limits. Through a gap in the trees, she caught a glimpse of the mountain where the plane had gone down. From this distance, it looked pristine.

Lenny had blown up the plane in the same spot she had originally planned. Just a half day later than expected, due to Heather Mayhew's detour to pick up Milan. When Lenny realized Milan would be on board, she had struggled with a sudden, illogical desire to find another way to eliminate her mother and her core staff.

Heather's inquiries had been discreet. She hadn't shared her unease via email, text, or phone. Just in person, to someone she trusted. Occasionally, Heather's phone was in her purse, and it was harder to listen from there. Luckily, like most people, Heather liked to have her phone in her hand. Even after she put Milan in the boarding school, she had texted her every day, sometimes multiple times.

Lenny hadn't been close to her own mom, who had died when she was eight. At the time, Lenny had thought Karl was truly mourning when he wiped his eyes at the funeral. Certainly, he had missed Sheila's presence. How she had kept things running smoothly at home. How she would cook his favorite noodle dish just the way his own mother had. But as Lenny got older, she realized Karl's sadness hadn't really been about Sheila's death, but more about how it affected him.

Although wasn't everyone just as selfish? Didn't death hurt because it impacted your life or because you imagined yourself in the dead person's shoes? Could you really mourn selflessly?

Maybe. It was surprising how much the thought of

Milan's death continued to bother Lenny. Long ago, she had rejected the thought of marriage, of children. She was lonely, yes, but she also knew she was fundamentally twisted, forever pulled between Karl and her own emotions, the ones she tried to deny.

Besides, it was foolish to have a family. Families were an easy way to get to someone. Point a gun at the head of their child and the target would do almost anything you asked, reveal any secret. You didn't even have to hurt the kid.

Usually.

Lenny rounded a corner. Ahead of her, going only about forty miles an hour, was a logging truck. She got right behind its bumper, staring at the round, perfectly straight tree trunks stacked like Lincoln Logs.

It slowed down to thirty-five. Despite the solid yellow line, she swung out into the oncoming lane. But an old blue truck appeared and she had to tuck back in again.

She must have sucked in a breath the wrong way, because the cough started up again. It took a minute to get the hacking under control. When it was finally finished, she wiped the back of her hand over her lips, then absently rubbed at the ache in her chest with two fingers.

Her navigation app said she still had three miles to go.

Once she reached the most logical spot, she would find the person with the phone. Discover what they knew, and then kill them. And then find Eric and kill him.

Take care of all the loose ends before the client took care of her.

Lenny put her hand on the steering wheel, ready to peek out from behind the truck again. On the back of her hand, a spot of color bloomed on the white skin.

Blood.

# Chapter 42

## MILAN
## ALIVE

MILAN STARTLED AWAKE WHEN THE WAITRESS SLIPPED THE receipt under her hand.

"You can't sleep here," Angel said. "This is a restaurant."

Just to spite her, Milan left a tip nearly equal to the bill.

She was so tired it was hard to walk the block to the Stay-A-While. The few cars in the motel's lot were older, and the building was in need of a paint job. Before she walked in, she pulled the hood farther over her head. A bell tinkled when she pushed open the door.

There was no one at the front desk. The top of the counter was cluttered with a bottle of hand sanitizer, an American flag the size of an index card, a ship in a bottle, a lamp with a yellow shade, a fake fern, and a rack with brochures showing happy people kayaking, hiking, or visiting a museum. From the wall, a stuffed moose head stared down at Milan. Below it, a row of hooks held keys. Only a few were empty. Maybe that lack of demand could work in her favor.

A man wearing a T-shirt and sweatpants stepped out of an open doorway behind the counter that led to what looked like a living area. He was young, with a scruffy beard and a backward baseball cap. He was running a paper towel over his lips, like he'd been in the middle of a meal.

She pitched her voice low. "Can I have a room for tonight?"

"One night?"

"Yeah." Milan fought the urge to make herself look smaller by slouching and keeping her arms tucked in. She stretched herself to her full length, with her legs wide and her arms akimbo. It was just like with the mountain lions. She needed to take up space.

"How many people?"

"Just me."

"Okay. I'll just need your ID and a credit card."

Her overfull stomach lurched. Milan had worried he wouldn't like her looks. She hadn't thought about having to show ID. "I don't have any ID. My wallet was, um, stolen."

He sighed. "Then how were you going to pay for the room?"

"I have cash." Milan put two fifties on the counter. She'd pulled them out of her pocket after leaving Denny's.

Skepticism colored his voice. "And they didn't get your cash when they stole your wallet?"

"I had it in a different pocket."

It was clearly a terrible lie. He didn't believe her. She could see it in the way his fingers hesitated over the keyboard.

"Please," she said, pushing the two fifties closer to him. "If you have to charge me more, that's okay."

After a long hesitation, he said, "One night. That's it." Milan didn't see where the two fifties disappeared to, but she didn't think it was the cash drawer.

"Thank you." Her voice came out too high and sounded too close to tears.

"Did you park in the lot? I'll need your license plate."

"I don't have a car."

She waited for him to push the money back, but he just sighed. "Okay. But no one else in your room. The stairs go right past that door"—he pointed at the door she'd just come in through—"so I'll know if you have anyone else up there. And if necessary, I will call the cops."

When she nodded, he took a key from one of the hooks and set it on the counter. It bore the number 214.

Back outside, it was all Milan could do to raise her feet high enough to clear the stairs.

The lock stuck, and it took a minute to get the key to

turn. The room was small, with a double bed. The carpet was a mottled red, the chair was upholstered in green, and the polyester bedspread was butter yellow. Despite the nonsmoking signs on both sides of the door, the room reeked of smoke.

It was paradise.

After making sure the curtains were tightly closed, Milan flipped the two extra locks on the door. She dropped the pilot's duffel on the bed and immediately headed for the bathroom. After using the toilet, she slowly stripped off her clothes and assessed the damage. Every piece of clothing she peeled off released a new, and more gamy, smell. Every inch of skin was bruised, blistered, dirty, scratched, or rubbed raw.

In comparison with the rest of her, her rainbow-colored broken finger, swollen to twice its normal size, didn't look worse than before. Her socks were stuck to her heels so firmly that she left them on when she got into the shower. The shower head was shorter than she was but she stayed in for a long time anyway, as if the water could wash away the images of death and destruction.

She was shivering, even though the shower was hot enough to redden her skin. She scrubbed herself all over with the tiny bar of soap and a washcloth so thin it was nearly see-through. She shampooed her hair three times. And then, slowly, she managed to peel off her socks. Her heels were like raw meat where blisters had formed, popped, and then been rubbed off. Even her toes were swollen, the skin strangely shiny.

Milan was a mess. But she was alive.

She just needed to stay that way.

# Chapter 43

## MILAN

# LIGHT ON THE OTHER SIDE

MILAN WOKE FROM A RESTLESS, PAINFUL SLEEP. IN THE MIDDLE OF the night, she had taken a few burning nips from the pilot's flask, but the liquor hadn't helped much. Every part of her ached: muscles, ligaments, tendons, even bones. It felt like the pain extended down to the cellular level. It hurt when she moved and when she lay still.

Her thoughts were sludgy, filled with the remnants of dreams she'd built from memories. The older ones had brought comfort. The newer ones had become nightmares.

There was light on the other side of the curtains. Morning, but just barely. She had to get up. She had to move. She wouldn't be safe until she retrieved whatever was in their home safe and took it to Mr. Kirkby.

Picking up the remote, Milan turned on CNN. They were talking about a snowstorm back east. The muscles in her legs cramped as she made her way to the bathroom.

In the mirror, still flecked with someone else's toothpaste, her eyes looked back at her from a stranger's face. A face that was harder, shadowed, expressionless. The bruises on her body were more colorful now: green, blue, reddish-brown. She'd slept in the pilot's remaining clean T-shirt.

From the TV, Milan heard her mother's name. When she ran back, her mom's picture was over the news anchor's shoulder.

"The body found at the site of a plane crash yesterday has been positively identified as that of Oregon senator Heather Mayhew. While there have been no reports of survivors, authorities say they have recovered remains.

"Heather Mayhew had only been in office for six months. She was elected to the seat previously held by her husband, the late senator Jack Mayhew, who died in a car accident last year.

"According to Heather Mayhew's office, the other people aboard the flight included the pilot, Maury Barth; her personal assistant, Jenna Spencer; her chief of staff, Eric Scott; her legislative director, Mark Smithee; and also the senator's sixteen-year-old daughter, Milan Mayhew."

Milan's picture from last year's yearbook flashed on the screen. "Witnesses reported that the plane touched down at a private terminal in Colorado to pick up Milan Mayhew from boarding school. The plane was headed for the senator's hometown of Portland. Senator Mayhew's Portland staff alerted authorities after they did not hear from her, and the plane was located yesterday afternoon.

"In a press conference, National Transportation Safety Board chair Michelle Pflegman said the 2003 turboprop crashed in Central Oregon's Cascade Mountains and then caught fire. The private plane did not have a black box recorder, but Pflegman said the cockpit voice recorder survived the crash. She said their plan is to recover every bit of wreckage and reassemble it to understand what happened. She did not answer questions about whether there was any connection between the crash and Senator Jack Mayhew's death six months ago in what has been considered an accident. In other news—"

The muscles in Milan's thighs were quivering, like she wanted to run or maybe fall down. Instead she switched off the TV and sat on the edge of the bed.

Had the authorities figured out that Eric never boarded the plane? Had the fire burned hot enough that they weren't sure whose remains they had?

Loneliness and isolation crested over her like a wave. No matter how impassive her face looked in the mirror, she was only sixteen.

Without giving herself time to think about whether it was a good idea, Milan picked up her phone and thumbed the power on. Eric would know what to do.

It was filled with dozens of text messages, at least one from pretty much everyone who had her number. One from Ms. Robbins that made her feel a stab of longing. But it was Chance's name she clicked on.

**Milan—please Milan tell me u r ok.**

**I'm so, so sorry. Can't believe I'll nvr see u again.**

**I nvr told u how much u meant to me.** Then he had typed a swear word, followed by: **I can't believe ur gone. I just can't.**

He had sent a selfie of the two of them on one of the Oregon Coast's rare hot days. Smiling, eyes squinting in the sun, they lay on their backs in the sand, the tops of their heads touching so they made a straight line.

The flood of memories and pain the photo unleashed left Milan barely able to breathe. She would never see her parents again, but what about Chance? Her mother had said Milan had to stay dead. But that didn't mean forever, did it? Her chest ached, as if her heart were literally breaking.

A tear dripped onto her phone's screen. Milan wanted so badly to reassure him, but instead she scrolled down to her messages with Eric. Right now she needed advice more than anything.

But her last text to Eric was still unread. What did that mean? Was he dead, too? Had they gotten to him before he could even see her warning?

In a panic, Milan powered off the phone. She wanted to read her other texts or more about the crash, or figure out how to get to Portland, but it wasn't safe.

She had already decided it wasn't safe to hitchhike in general, and in her case in particular. And while Harold had clearly wanted to help, that probably didn't extend to driving her to Portland and not asking any questions. That left the bus, only she didn't know the schedule or even where the station was.

How did people figure things out before the internet? Phone? The motel's square brown plastic phone was as big as a toaster, the handset you both talked into and listened to connected to the body with a curly cord. In the night-stand drawer she found a phone book. In old novels, phone books were sometimes used as booster seats, but this one was barely an inch thick.

When she picked up the phone to call Greyhound, the heft of the handset was surprising. They said the bus to Portland would be leaving in an hour and forty minutes. She had to hurry.

It still seemed safer to walk through the world as a man, or at least a guy. Back in the bathroom she used the pilot's nail scissors to hack at her hair, quickly learning she had to keep the sections small. For once she was thankful her hair wasn't thick. Now all the blue was gone and the remaining hair was about three inches long. She used the pilot's hair gel to slick it back. Last night, she'd even used his toothbrush to brush her teeth. Now she did it again.

At least she had her own underwear. She pulled on a pair of brown cords, then topped them again with the pilot's pants. She started to put on a clean bra, then stopped. Breasts were kind of a giveaway, even under a sweatshirt. She cut the crotch out of a pair of underwear, then pulled the tube of fabric over her head. It definitely made her flatter. For once Milan was grateful that, like her hair, she was pretty average in that department. She added a long-sleeved shirt, then a fleece.

Her Columbia coat looked too much like a woman's coat. Reluctantly, she shoved it in the pilot's duffel. As she did, she touched the hard outline of the gun in the separate pocket. After a moment's hesitation, she put the gun in her sweatshirt pouch, then checked the mirror.

The lump was pretty obvious, even if you couldn't tell exactly what was making it. She returned it to the duffel. Yesterday's clothes went in the garbage can, on top of her chopped-off hair.

Milan had just zipped up the duffel when a knock on the door made her jump.

"Housekeeping," a woman's voice called out. It held the trace of an accent.

# Chapter 44

## LENNY
# FULL BLAST

LENNY KNOCKED ON THE DOOR. "HOUSEKEEPING," SHE CALLED OUT, adopting the accent of someone who spoke English as a second language.

Whoever now possessed Milan's phone had turned it on for a little over a minute, just long enough to check the text messages. The location software had been able to pinpoint the phone's location to within a hundred meters. Those hundred meters pretty much corresponded with the footprint of the Stay-A-While Motel. The motel was cheap and looked it. Not even an elevator. But which room was the target in?

Wearing a wig and sunglasses, Lenny had walked into the office, a bell ringing over her head. No one was at the front desk, but behind it a wooden numbered board with hooks for keys had only four blank spots. She left before the clerk came out.

Her running shoes soundless on the stairs, Lenny headed upstairs first. She took a quick survey, prepared to tie up the actual housekeeper, but saw no one. The place was so dead it probably didn't make sense to pay one, at least not every day.

But dead was good. Dead meant less chance of witnesses who might also need to wind up dead.

Given the lack of an elevator, there must be cleaning supplies on both floors. There was only one unmarked door. Lenny quickly picked the lock. As she had guessed, it was a workroom, complete with a washer, dryer, and wheeled cart. Wire shelves held toilet paper, towels, bins of tiny toiletries, and a stack of folded uniforms. Lenny slid her arms into a navy smock and pulled it on over her black turtleneck and jeans. The move made her jeans threaten to slide off her hips, and she hauled them up with one hand. The fake pregnancy belly meant she had to leave the last few buttons of the smock unbuttoned. Careful not to touch the box, she grabbed a pair of cheap blue vinyl gloves and pulled them on.

The first room that had had a missing key was 216. Lenny knocked on the door and called out "Housekeeping!" She felt like a runner in the blocks, waiting for the starter's gun. But there was no answer, even when she knocked a second time.

The flimsy lock was just as easy to pick as the one for the workroom had been. She eased the door open, braced to find someone sleeping, but the room was empty. It was also a sty, with clothes and food wrappers littering every available surface. It smelled like feet and old french fries. The occupant must be living here and, by the looks of things, must have been for weeks. It was lucky for both of them that they weren't home.

The next room with a missing key was 214. Lenny repeated her knock and call, her scalp tingling under her wig. She already knew this room was different.

"I don't need anything," a hoarse voice called out. "I'll be checking out soon."

Lenny knocked again. "Do you need new towels?"

Then the door opened. "No, I don't need anything."

At first Lenny thought she had again found the wrong room. But then she processed what she was seeing. Milan. Dressed to look like a boy. Although no boy should have eyes that haunted. Eyes that had clearly seen too much.

Milan! How had a kid managed to do everything she'd done?

Lenny shoved the cart into the room, then stepped in and kicked the door closed behind her. Before Milan could react, Lenny grabbed her shoulder with her left hand. With her right, she pressed a gun into the girl's abdomen.

"I won't hurt you," she lied. "All I need to know is what your mother told you before she died." Her eyes cut past the duffel bag on the bed to the old brown phone squatting on the night table. She knew what Milan had done on her cell phone, but could she have called someone?

Milan lunged. Not toward the door, but back. She reached for the phone's handset.

Lenny had to stop the girl before she called for help.

But she had completely misread the situation. Like a Spanish gaucho whirling a bolo, Milan grabbed the curly cord and spun the handset in a circle over her head.

Before Lenny could process what was happening, the handset crashed into her left cheekbone and eye socket. She gasped in shock as tears sprang into her left eye, blurring her vision. Milan whipped the phone again. This time the cord wrapped itself around Lenny's neck, half strangling her. The handset thumped the back of her head.

Milan darted past her. But she didn't run out of the room. Instead she snatched up a bottle of cleaning fluid from the cart and sprayed it right in Lenny's eyes.

As Lenny let out an involuntary scream and clawed at her face, she heard the girl grab the duffel bag, open the door, and run out.

Momentarily blinded, Lenny fumbled toward the bathroom only to be pulled up short by the telephone cord. Her fingers clawed at her throat as she struggled to free herself, her eyes and nose streaming. Finally she managed to unwrap it. Hands outstretched so she wouldn't run into anything, she staggered into the bathroom, stuck her face under the faucet, and turned the sink on full blast.

Who had trained Milan? Because the Mayhew kid was clearly an operative.

# Chapter 45

JANIE

# BIG BLACK BOX

**Two years earlier**

JANIE HAD LOST TWO COWS AND A CALF WHEN SHE HEARD ABOUT a scientist, Floyd Higgins, who worked at a private testing lab. He was widely regarded as a bit of an eccentric who used words no one knew, and spent his limited time away from the lab fishing and reading science fiction. From the beginning, Floyd had been outspoken in his belief that fracking was a mistake. That hadn't endeared him to anyone local.

Floyd told Janie to meet him in a park in the next town over, and to bring her grandkids for cover. When he joined her on the park bench, he was wearing a baseball cap pulled low over his eyes. He was in his midfifties, with a belly that strained at the front of his plaid shirt. But under the bill of his cap, his eyes were alert and intelligent.

Janie told him about how everything was changing. "I'm pasturing my cows on what I always have: rye, orchard grass, tall fescue, white clover. It is the same feed, but their yield is way down. They're not breeding like they should. And they're eating twice as much, but they just keep losing weight."

Before driving over, Janie had walked into the paddock. The cows had regarded her with deeply sunken eyes. One was even shaking her head from side to side, a motion that didn't seem voluntary.

Floyd nodded. "Animals live outside, breathing the air and drinking directly from ponds, streams, puddles. And with their shorter reproductive cycles, toxin-induced infertility manifests sooner."

"What does that mean?" Ideally a dairy cow had a calf a year, but some of Janie's cows hadn't gotten pregnant in close to two.

"In other words, if nature is polluted, the animals show it first."

Janie's mouth suddenly tasted bitter. She pulled a canning jar full of dirty water from her big purse, similar to the one she had given to Steve Hamill. "I'll pay you to test this for me. Maybe then Prospect will believe me about the water turning bad." She would use the last of the money she had gotten from them. It seemed like karma.

"Do you think they'll listen? That anyone will listen?" Floyd lifted an eyebrow as bushy as a caterpillar. "No one wants to hear what I have to tell them."

"And what's that?" Janie's heart was knocking in her chest. She looked at Noelle and Darcy climbing the big colorful plastic play structure. Did she really want to know?

"That what's happening under their land is a big black box. Back when George W. Bush was president, Vice President Cheney pushed an energy bill through Congress. It not only exempted fracking from the Safe Drinking Water Act but also allowed drillers to claim whatever they're injecting is a trade secret. Do you know what they use to frack?"

Janie repeated what Steve had told her. "Water, sand, a few chemicals."

"Sometimes the smallest things can do the most damage." Floyd scanned the parking lot before he continued. "They're using literally hundreds of chemicals to coax out more gas. But I think Prospect is using some kind of PFAS." He pronounced it *pee-fas*. "Fluorine-related carbon compounds. They don't occur in nature. They have to be manufactured, and there are hundreds, maybe thousands, of them. In the forties and fifties they started using them to make things like waterproof jackets, Teflon pans, and stain-resistant carpeting. Better living through chemistry, right? People thought they were as safe as soap. Only now we know they just stay in your body. Some people call them forever chemicals, because they don't break down. They've been linked to cancer, thyroid disease, immune system disorders, birth defects...."

"Birth defects?" Janie echoed weakly. Becca was pregnant, this time with a boy. She and Thad were over the moon. They were planning to name him Bart.

"The EPA is starting to say the safe level of these PFAS is vanishingly small, like one grain of sand in fifty Olympic-sized swimming pools. Whatever this chemical is, I'm finding it at a hundred times that or more."

"Where? Where are you finding it?"

He gave his head a little shake. "Everyplace. But especially in tap water, groundwater, and wells near where Prospect Power is fracking."

Janie felt faint. Every time she put on a pot of coffee, boiled spaghetti, or told her grandkids to brush their teeth before bed, was she actually poisoning her family?

"So you're thinking Prospect is using this chemical?"

Floyd leaned forward and lowered his voice. "What I need is proof. Proof that what's in the fracking fluid they're shooting into the ground is what's turning up in people's wells, coming out of taps in town." He looked at her. "I wasn't going to meet with you, until you mentioned your son-in-law works for Prospect. I need him to get my hands on some of that fluid. With it, I can connect the dots."

# Chapter 46

## MILAN
# THE TRICK

AS THE PREGNANT WOMAN WITH THE GUN CLAWED AT HER EYES with her free hand, Milan dropped the spray bottle and shouldered past her, grabbing the duffel on the way. After throwing open the door, she hurtled down the stairs, past the motel's office, and into the parking lot.

What if that woman had an accomplice waiting for her? Just like with the mountain lions, running would draw attention. Would make Milan look like prey. But she didn't have any choice. She had to put some distance between herself and the woman who wanted to kill her. Only where could she go?

Milan ran across the four lanes of highway, ignoring

the sound of horns. Sprinting past the pumps, she ran toward the mini-mart behind the gas station.

A woman had just tried to kill her. A woman, and a pregnant one at that. How could you be growing a new life in your belly while you were trying to take another?

And how had the woman found her? It must have been through her phone. Without breaking stride, Milan pulled it from her pocket and tossed it in the trash can outside the store.

Should she run inside, beg the clerk to call the police? But how long would it take them to come? And even if they did, what then?

Again, she heard her mom's words. *Don't trust anyone.* Not even a pregnant woman in a cleaner's outfit. In her head, Milan dubbed the woman Nikita, after the assassin in a TV show her parents had liked. Because that had clearly been her goal—to kill Milan.

Her heart rabbiting in her chest, her breath coming in gasps, Milan cut behind the store, past a loading dock, and over a weedy patch of ground.

Now she was on a more residential street. But she was also alone. No other pedestrians. What had Nikita done with the real housekeeper, the one who should have been pushing that cart? Had she killed her? Milan's breath shook. Her mouth tasted like blood.

She hurried down the block, panting, pressing her

good hand into a stitch in her side. Ahead, a white car turned onto the street. She ducked behind some arborvitae and watched it pass, her heart pounding. The driver, an old woman with white hair, stared straight ahead.

But what if Nikita had simply donned a white wig? In the hotel room, it had looked like she might have been wearing one. Even after the car turned the corner, Milan waited another minute before coming out from behind the hedge.

The road she was on ran parallel to the main road. Milan thought she was heading in the general direction of the bus station. Not knowing what else to do, she kept hurrying forward under the charcoal gray sky, memories swamping her.

Mark, his eyes open and dull. The headless pilot, now revealed to be Maury. Jenna wreathed in flames, screaming. The life leaving her mother's face. The white world of the tree well. The mountain lions' yellow eyes and shining fangs.

And finally Nikita, her face contorting as the spray hit her eyes.

The first drops of rain hit Milan's face. After pulling her coat out of the duffel, she realized wearing it was a good idea. Nikita hadn't seen it. It would make Milan look at least a little different from how she had in the motel. But that probably wasn't enough. And the cut made her look like a girl.

After a half dozen more blocks, she went back toward

the main road. In addition to four lanes of cars, there was also more foot traffic around the stores lining both sides of the street.

On the next block was something called Bend Bargains. It seemed like a combination thrift/junk store. Lined up under the overhanging roof were a desk, an upholstered chair, and several filing cabinets with wooden chairs set on top. Milan ducked inside.

It was so crowded with display cases and racks that she felt even more overwhelmed. Gritting her teeth, she pushed past shelves so full of knickknacks that the ceramic angels, nesting dolls, and plastic vases were in danger of tumbling off. She headed straight toward the racks of clothes. A pair of blue scrub pants caught her eye. They had a drawstring waist, so they would surely fit. She pulled out the hanger. In vain, she ran her hand down the line of shirts, first the women's and then the men's, looking for a matching scrub top. Nothing. She grabbed a plain white long-sleeved tee and a plain pink short-sleeved tee, both a little big. If she layered them over each other and paired them with the scrub pants, she might look like a nurse.

"Do you have a dressing room?" she asked the salesgirl behind the counter.

The girl, who had dyed red hair and a hoop in her nose, looked up from her phone. She pointed toward a corner. "In the back."

Along the way, Milan grabbed a black backpack. The

pilot's duffel was distinctive, and Nikita might remember it. Just before she pulled back the curtain to the dressing room, she spotted one more thing. An ash blond wig styled to look like the ends of the hair had been dyed violet. Two could play at the wig game.

Five minutes later Milan walked up to the counter, dressed as her new persona. Close up, if she tipped her head down, the staples in the crown of the wig were visible. But from even a few feet away, it looked like real hair. Well, actually like a real bad dye job. Milan thought she could pass for, perhaps not a nurse, but maybe an aide who worked in an old folks' home.

Maybe the trick was simply believing you were really what you presented. Whether it was male or a nurse or whatever. After all, Milan hadn't thought twice about the "housekeeper" until she drew her gun.

"I'd like to buy these. I'm already wearing them." She laid down all the sales tags. "And donate these." With a thump, she set the pilot's duffel on the counter. It was now filled with the clothes she'd been wearing at the motel, including the makeshift binder. The gun was now in the backpack.

"Um, okay." The salesgirl's brow furrowed, but she just rang everything up without asking questions. Milan paid from her dwindling store of cash.

As the girl put the change in her hand, Milan hesitated.

But the risk of this girl knowing her plans was less than the risk of wandering around lost.

"Could you tell me how to get to the bus station?"

Before she answered, the girl pressed her lips together. Her eyes went from Milan's broken finger to the wig and then back to Milan's face. It looked like she had guessed Milan was on the run, although surely not from what. Then the girl gave her directions.

The bus station was less than a half mile away. As she walked out into the pattering rain, Milan put on her coat, pulled up her hood, and, with a wince, stuck her bad hand in her pocket.

# Chapter 47

LENNY

# TRIGGER

THE MOTEL'S TOWELS WERE SO THIN THEY SEEMED TO ACTUALLY repel water rather than dry Lenny's face. As she washed the spray cleaner out of her eyes, her wig slid off. Now her hair was plastered to her head.

Lenny blinked rapidly and then tried to focus. While her eyes still burned and her vision was watery, she thought the cleaner Milan had sprayed into her face hadn't done any permanent damage.

She hoped.

Clearly, she had dramatically underestimated the girl. She'd bought into the "boarding school" story, but had that been a cover? She had come into this motel room expecting a garden hose and instead discovered a snake.

Belatedly, Lenny realized that back out in the room, the door was still open.

She walked toward it, her hair dripping on the carpet. As she started to close the door, a young guy in a backward baseball cap was reaching the top of the stairs.

"I heard you guys. What did I say about having guests," he said. It wasn't a question. Then he took a closer look at Lenny, with her fake belly and blue vinyl gloves. "Who in the heck are you?"

Her trigger finger itched, but her gun was still back on the bathroom counter. That stupid girl had rattled her.

Just as he was reaching the second floor's concrete walkway, Lenny took two running steps and grabbed the handrail. She leaped, launching her body like an arrow aimed straight at the motel clerk. The bottoms of her tennis shoes connected with the center of his chest.

With a shout, he fell back, arms pinwheeling. Only her grip on the handrail kept her from sailing after him.

Back in the room, she grabbed her gun and wig and left, taking the stairs two at a time.

At the bottom, the guy was trying to sit up, groaning. When he saw Lenny he shrank back. A thin trickle of blood oozed from where he'd bit his lip, but otherwise there were no obvious injuries. His wide, frightened eyes darted back and forth between her fake pregnancy and her gun.

Lenny's finger tightened on the trigger. She weighed

her options in a split second. If she shot the clerk, he wouldn't be able to tell the cops a thing about her or Milan.

Then again, if she didn't shoot him, it seemed likely that any statement he gave to the cops would focus on her gun and her belly, the two things currently transfixing him. He clearly wasn't that observant, since he'd thought Lenny was Milan. Although now that she thought about it, she and Milan weren't that physically dissimilar.

If she killed him, then this would be murder and not simple assault. The cops would go over the room, cart, and janitor's closet with a fine-toothed comb. Lenny had probably left some kind of DNA in or around the sink—snot, hair, tears. She'd even spit out some of the cleanser that had landed in her mouth.

Her finger relaxed and she jumped over him. In a few steps, she was around the corner and out of sight.

And then Lenny's luck turned.

Her phone vibrated. She didn't recognize the number but still answered it.

And at the sound of the voice on the other end of the line, Lenny smiled.

# Chapter 48

## MILAN
## DISTRACTION

MILAN HURRIED TO THE GREYHOUND STATION. WITHOUT HER phone, she didn't know what time it was. Had she missed the bus to Portland?

To her relief, the bus was still there, idling out front. The driver stood between the steps and the open luggage compartment. He checked the ticket of the young Black guy at the front of the line. Then he picked up his suitcase and slotted it into the bottom of the bus as the passenger went up the stairs.

Was she too late to buy a ticket? Inside, an electronic reader board showed the bus wouldn't leave for another fifteen minutes. A half dozen people stood in line for the one female clerk who was working, and Milan got behind them. According to the board, the trip from Bend to downtown Portland would take three and a half hours, but at least it also said it was nonstop.

"I'll just need to see your ID," the clerk said to the woman she was helping.

As the customer dug in her purse, Milan could feel her heartbeat in her ears, her fingertips. What was she going to do?

With a sour, impatient expression, the clerk waited for the older woman to produce her license. She did not look like she would accept Milan's lie about a stolen wallet. Those narrowed eyes would immediately clock that her hair was a wig. The clerk might even realize the face under it belonged to a girl on the news, a girl who was supposed to be dead.

At a minimum, Milan would draw a lot of attention to herself, and even then she probably wouldn't be able to buy a ticket.

But if she didn't get on the bus, how would she get to Portland? Nikita was not going to stop hunting her.

Milan went back outside. Even when the driver pushed a suitcase under the bus, he still kept an eye on the line. There was no way she could sneak past him and on board. She pretended to be looking inside her backpack. Again she was startled by the sight of the gun.

The driver slotted another suitcase into place. Milan had to get on the bus.

Or maybe not *on* exactly. What about the luggage compartment? But the driver was right next to it.

She needed a distraction.

Her gaze snagged on the wire-mesh trash can halfway between the bus and the terminal. At the bottom was a crumpled newspaper. As if tying her shoe, she knelt beside the trash, hoping no one noticed she was wearing pull-on boots. After taking her lighter from her pocket, she flicked the wheel and set the wavering yellow flame to the newspaper. It caught but didn't whoosh into a pillar of flame the way she had hoped. Gently, she blew on the tiny flickers, enough that they grew bigger but not so hard that she blew them out.

Had it only been a few days ago that lighting paper on fire had led to her being on her mother's plane? Had led to her being the only survivor of a plane crash, chased by a killer?

The fire strengthened. Milan got to her feet. The flames were starting to climb past the top of the trash can.

No one else noticed.

Finally she said to the last guy in line, "Hey, look at that fire."

"Fire?" he echoed. Then he turned, saw it, and shouted, "Fire!"

The driver leaped up the steps to the bus, grabbed a fire extinguisher from under his seat, and ran toward the flames. Everyone began shouting and milling around, some getting closer and some backing away. But all eyes were on the fire.

While they were distracted, Milan slid into the luggage hold, clambering behind all the other suitcases and boxes. Once there, she froze, barely daring to breathe.

Eventually the commotion calmed down, more luggage came clonking in, and the doors to the luggage compartment banged closed.

A few minutes later they were pulling out of the station.

# Chapter 49

# MILAN
# RABID DOG

HIDDEN IN THE LUGGAGE COMPARTMENT, MILAN ARMY-CRAWLED toward the front of the bus, trying to get away from the area closest to the tailpipe. It still smelled of diesel up here, but not as strongly. It was hard not to feel claustrophobic. The space wasn't tall enough for her to fully sit up. Her roof was the bus passengers' floor.

They were on the freeway now. Between the engine and the tires, it was so loud. Milan lay with her head propped up on someone's soft-sided suitcase. In a little over three hours, they would be in Portland. And then what?

Once it was dark, she could use her dad's keys to sneak into her house through the back door. In the basement, she'd open the safe and find the information that had led to the deaths of so many people. And then she'd make her way to Brent's house with it. Make sure he was alone before she revealed that she was alive and what she had.

The key ring! Not only did it hold the keys to the house and the safe, but the car fob must be for the Prius. The car would be safer and faster than walking or taking the bus.

Milan must have dozed off. She woke to a world without the rumble of the engines. The doors on the luggage compartment slid up and suddenly light shone through the gaps. When the big suitcase between her and the door moved, she took her chance. Feet first, she scooted out after it, one hand holding her backpack and the other clamped on her wig.

"Hey!" someone shouted behind Milan as she started running. "Come back here!"

Milan kept running. Her left leg, the one that had been broken in the car accident, was stiff, so it was more of a hobble. But no one tackled her. It probably wasn't worth it to them to risk a physical confrontation.

It was early afternoon. She had about four hours before the sun set. The main branch of the public library was about a twenty-minute walk away. Milan set off. As she passed a Mexican food cart, her stomach grumbled. Her last meal had been at Denny's. She ordered a chicken burrito, nearly as big as a football and wrapped in foil, as well as a Diet Coke for the caffeine.

After sitting on a low wall, Milan unwrapped the

burrito and forced herself to eat it slowly. It was delicious. The chicken was juicy, the rice tender, and the sauce had just the right amount of heat.

Finished, Milan sat for a long moment, trying to empty her mind, to just appreciate the weak sunshine on her face. But she couldn't stop thinking. *What kind of information is bad enough that so many people died for it?*

According to her mom, it had originally been given to her dad. His election platform had been built on protecting the environment, especially limiting the use of fossil fuels. Maybe he had been given secret evidence of a coal company illegally slicing off the tops of mountains, or offshore drilling killing manatees?

Milan tossed her trash and then started for the library. Once she entered the high-ceilinged, hushed space, with its grand wooden staircase, she headed for the room that held rows and rows of computers. She found an empty chair in a far corner, well away from other users, and slipped on the pair of headphones resting on top of the monitor.

Once she got online, she googled her mom's name, then read article after article.

*"Authorities now believe at least one person initially survived the crash. Rescuers are scouring the mountainside, but the terrain is tricky and the weather is not cooperating."*

One link was to a TV story labeled "Breaking News." When Milan clicked, two women seated behind a desk appeared. In a corner of the screen was her mom's picture.

The woman with box braids said, "We're just learning of a surprising twist in the investigation into Senator Heather Mayhew's plane crash. Authorities are said to be reexamining Senator Jack Mayhew's car accident."

Her mom's photo was replaced by her dad's.

"Why would they do that?" the woman with the blond bob said.

"Authorities have started doing the math about this spate of seeming accidents." Box Braids nodded, setting them swinging. "The common denominator they all have is Milan Mayhew."

Now Milan's picture replaced her dad's. Milan drew the front strands of her wig forward, obscuring even more of her face.

"What do you mean?" Blond Bob's brows drew together.

"Just look at her troubled history. In addition to being present for this horrific plane crash, who was sitting next to Jack Mayhew when his car inexplicably careened out of its lane? It's even come out that Milan told first responders her dad's accident was her fault. Did she attack him and cause him to lose control? As for the plane, could she have assaulted the pilot?" Box Braids sounded delighted by these possibilities.

Blond Bob was more skeptical. "But wait a minute—isn't the door to the cockpit locked?"

"You're thinking of a commercial airliner. But this was

a private plane. There's only a curtain between the pilot and the rest of the plane. And the only reason Milan Mayhew was on the plane was because she had been expelled from boarding school. Which is the *third* boarding school that has kicked her out for disruptive behavior. We've heard from a source at the most recent school that she actually set fire to her own belongings, and that fire then spread to the rest of the school. What we might be looking at is a troubled teen who is trying to harm herself and anyone else in her vicinity."

Blond Bob tilted her head. "So a girl with a death wish?"

"Who was willing to let others die," Box Braids chimed in.

Milan's blood turned to ice. Someone was determined to make her out to be a killer. A sociopath.

A rabid dog that needed to be put down.

Chapter 50

LENNY

# OVERSIGHT

WHEN SHE HADN'T BEEN ABLE TO FIND MILAN OUTSIDE THE MOTEL, Lenny had taken preventative measures. Parked in the far corner of a Walmart parking lot, thumbs moving furiously over her phone's keyboard, she had seeded a story in the dark corners of the internet, knowing it wouldn't be long until it made its way to the mainstream. Just as she finished, her phone rang. She didn't need to look at the display to know who it was.

"Yes." The cough threatened to bubble up again, but Lenny swallowed it. She couldn't afford to seem weak. She'd fluffed her hair over her forehead to hide the bruise the phone's handset had left. Luckily her turtleneck covered the red lines from where the cord had bit into her throat.

"I'm hearing there might have been survivors from the crash." The client bit off the words. "How is that possible?"

"The pilot was ex-military. He managed to bring the plane down more or less in one piece. But Heather is definitely dead. And I'm already on their trail."

Lenny left out the part about Milan already having managed to evade her. And if she took care of Eric soon, the client might never need to learn Eric hadn't actually boarded the plane in the first place.

He grunted. "We have to stop this thing before it metastasizes. I don't need any loose ends. So you're getting some help."

Lenny stilled. "What do you mean?"

"I called in someone else. His name is Roscoe. He'll be in Portland soon."

Lenny hadn't met Roscoe, but she'd heard of him. He had a reputation as a cowboy, a daredevil. And when it came to women, his definition of "taking care of things" was rumored to be . . . overzealous.

This day had already held too many surprises. Gritting her teeth, she took a beat before answering. "You know I prefer to work alone." The only person she trusted to do things right was herself.

"You can't be everywhere at once. Tell Roscoe what to do, and he'll do it. Just think of him as another pair of hands."

Or another pair of eyes—on her. Lenny gripped the

phone with such force she heard it creak. "I'd really prefer to take care of things myself."

"I'm afraid we've already moved to plan B. I'll text you his number."

The client didn't like to get his hands dirty. And he wanted his spotless reputation to stay that way.

Lenny made a noise like agreement and then disconnected. She was sure Roscoe was already figuring out how to, at a minimum, make her look bad. Or more than likely, kill her. Why work with Lenny when instead he could be the new Lenny?

So how could she use him before he used her?

Lenny started cruising the streets again, looking for Milan.

Could the girl simply be an innocent who'd just been lucky enough to survive a crash and a trek through the wilderness? Lenny snorted at the thought. Heather must have gotten her only daughter private lessons with someone like Karl.

And now Milan was in the wind. So where would the kid—Lenny now used the term loosely—go? What had her mother told her to do?

Clearly, it hadn't been to call the police. And surely not to stay in Bend. No, Milan would be trying to get to Portland. Either to share the information or to retrieve it. The information the client had paid Lenny a lot of money to make disappear.

At a minimum, Portland's streets would be familiar and there would be at least a few friendly faces. Although that number should be dwindling. Lenny had just seen to that.

So how would Milan try to get home? Hitching would be risky, both in terms of who picked her up and having to wait out in the open. Flying would mean having to provide her name to the authorities. Even if she got past them, she would have to wait at the small airport, where you could count on there always being a TV blaring CNN. Even taking Amtrak or Greyhound would require an ID.

By the time Lenny spotted the charred trash can in front of the Greyhound bus station, the bus to Portland had been gone over an hour. When she heard about the pandemonium the fire had caused, a grudging admiration filled her. Milan must have slipped on board when everyone's attention was elsewhere. But it was too late for Lenny to catch up, even if she sped the whole way.

After calling Roscoe, Lenny explained some of the plan to him. Not all. She would keep pieces in her back pocket, ready for emergencies.

"I can get to the bus station before it arrives." Lenny had plugged her phone into the dash, and Roscoe's voice came through the car's speakers. "If I spot her, what do you want me to do?"

"First, we don't need her to be arrested, so if someone realizes she snuck on board, you need to make sure no one detains her. And if you see her try to call or meet up with someone, nip that in the bud. Otherwise, just hold back and see what she does."

When Lenny was still an hour outside Portland, Roscoe called back.

"She just came sliding out of the luggage compartment. She ran off and they didn't try to chase her. I'll send you a pic. She's changed clothes. And she's wearing a wig."

Lenny mentally tipped her hat to riding in the luggage compartment. When her phone dinged, she cut her eyes back and forth between the road and the screen. The wig made Milan look older, and the layered, loose clothes hid the shape of her body. She squinted. Whoever trained her hadn't taught her that a tracker always looked at the shoes, knowing people would often change everything but them. Milan still had on her black boots.

Lenny spent the rest of the drive making a series of phone calls, putting the rest of her plan into motion.

By the time she got into Portland, Roscoe was in the public library, in a seat two rows away from Milan. He reported that all she had done was check news coverage of herself. She hadn't emailed anyone, she hadn't spoken to anyone.

And when Roscoe texted to say Milan was on the move, Lenny went to the one place everyone went when they were in trouble.

Home.

Not hers, of course.

Milan's.

# Chapter 51

MILAN

# INTO THE DARKNESS

WITHOUT HER PHONE, MILAN COULDN'T CHECK HER TEXTS. BUT SHE could, she realized, check her email. And when she logged in to her email provider from the library's computer, there were nearly as many messages as there had been texts.

But with one crucial difference. When she scrolled down, there was a message with the subject line "Read Me First" from someone with the username Betcha$1.

How many times had Eric said that phrase to her? Pulse quickening, Milan clicked.

Milan—are you okay? When I heard you might have survived, I couldn't believe it. Thank God. Thank God. But I hope you see this before you do anything. You need to lie low. Whatever you do, do NOT go to the authorities. It's not safe.

Your mom asked me to check out some evidence she found in your dad's things, and I went to the FBI. Forty-eight hours later, someone blows up her plane. I don't think that's a coincidence. I'm on my way back to Portland. When I get there, we can figure out what to do.

Milan put a hand over her eyes, hiding her tears from the other patrons. She wasn't alone.

She started to hit the button to reply but then hesitated. Could someone be monitoring her email, either the authorities or the bad guys? Or were they one and the same?

Right now, maybe it was enough knowing that Eric was on his way to Portland. Once she was at Mr. Kirkby's and knew more, she could email Eric back.

By the time the light from the library windows was starting to dim, it took all of Milan's energy to push back her chair and get to her feet. It would take about forty-five minutes to walk home. The thought of riding the bus was tempting. But what if someone she knew was on it or a stranger recognized her from the news? No, on foot was better. Along the way, she took off the wig, which felt increasingly itchy, and put it in her backpack.

Once she was in her neighborhood, Milan felt like she had the advantage. This was her turf. No outsider would know what she knew—who had a dog or a security camera, who always kept an eye on the window, whose yard she could cut across with impunity. As she made her way through Mrs. Littlefield's big backyard, it was tempting to knock on her door. She always had fresh-baked cookies. And she would never rat out Milan.

Milan hopped over the low wall separating their two backyards. In her black coat, she moved from shadow to shadow. Nothing seemed out of place, and she was the only one outside.

The yard was neat, thanks to the lawn service. The roof was mostly solar panels that absorbed the light and reflected nothing back. At the end of their long driveway sat her mom's Prius. Milan touched the fob in her pocket. In a few minutes she would have whatever was hidden in the safe, and then she would get in the car and drive away.

Across the street, Chance's bedroom light was on. At the sight of a shadow moving on the other side of the curtain, a wave of dizziness passed over her. A year ago, Milan might have been in that room with him, studying or talking. Now she was on the run, her parents were dead, and people were speculating it was all her fault. Chance must know how crazy that idea was.

Milan walked up the back porch, her dad's key at the ready. Even if she hadn't had it, the third rock from the right probably still hid a spare. The key slipped into the lock. When she stepped inside, an alarm started buzzing. She almost jumped out of her skin. But her fingers automatically went to the lighted keypad and picked out the four digits of her birthday. A split second later, it was silent again.

For a moment, she didn't move, seeing if the sound had elicited any response. Inside and out, everything was still.

The air smelled stale, but it also smelled like home. Behind her was the back door. To her right, the kitchen. And directly ahead of her were the stairs to the basement, where the safe was. Milan slid the bolt to one side, pulled open the door, and descended into the darkness.

# Chapter 52

# MILAN
# CAUGHT IN A MAZE

MORE THAN ANYTHING, MILAN WANTED TO TURN AROUND, GO upstairs to her room, curl up on her bed, and fall asleep. Instead she pulled the basement door closed behind her, then turned on the light at the top of the stairs.

In addition to the washer and dryer, the basement was mostly filled with seasonal items—lawn chairs, a croquet set, a barbecue, boxes of Christmas ornaments. This last Christmas, her mom hadn't even bothered to decorate.

The safe was set into the wall directly across from the stairway, next to the electrical panel and above her dad's workbench. From the ring of keys, Milan selected the small brass one. She slid it in, holding her breath. It fit and she turned it.

Her mother's faint whisper echoed in her head. *Evidence . . . inside. Give to Brent.*

The door swung open. Inside were three black velvet jewelry boxes and a neat stack of file folders and manila envelopes, all labeled in her mother's handwriting.

Milan would never read anything new written by her mom.

She spread the folders over the clean surface of the workbench. None was helpfully labeled "Evidence that could get you killed." Instead they all bore practical notations: "Insurance," "Birth certificates," "Wedding license," "Warranties," "House deed."

There were also three fat manilla envelopes of photos, labeled "Jack's family," "Heather's family," and simply "Our family."

But that was it. Milan opened the jewelry boxes. The diamond earrings her dad had given her mom on their anniversary. Her grandma's wedding and engagement rings. And a pearl necklace she couldn't remember seeing her mom ever wear.

Had someone been here before her? Taken whatever it was?

Working more slowly, she opened each folder and inspected the contents. But everything was just what the labels said: receipts, documents, paperwork.

If she went to Mr. Kirkby empty-handed, could he even help her?

Milan undid the metal fastener on the envelope marked "Our family" and shook out the photos. Christmases, birthdays, vacations. These weightless little squares were all she had left of her family.

They were mostly of her. On her first birthday, her face smeared with chocolate. At five, sitting under a Christmas tree and holding up a stuffed rabbit. A helmet-clad seven-year-old Milan astride a pony, eyes wide as if it might start bucking. A thirteen-year-old Milan dressed in a black halter dress. Her mom hadn't wanted her to wear it, but Milan had ultimately prevailed. At the time, she had thought it made her look very grown up, but she now saw that it emphasized how young she was.

She would give anything to have her parents back, nagging and cajoling.

Tears stung her eyes. Not only did strangers want to kill her, but other people were calling her a killer.

And it had taken every bit of ingenuity and bravery she had to get here, only to find nothing.

She rested her head in her hands, too tired to even think what to do next.

A voice behind her made her jump. "Hello, Milan."

She turned as a woman stepped out from behind the water heater, on the far side of the washer and dryer. It was Nikita, only with different hair and no baby bump. It must have been just as fake as the wig.

She still had the same gun, though.

And even worse, now another voice, a man's, came from the top of the stairs. "Someone call for backup?"

A cop about her dad's age bounded down the wooden stairs. He had dark hair and a high forehead. And his gun was pointed right at her heart.

As she raised her hands, Milan babbled, "You have to help me. This woman tried to kill me." She pointed at Nikita with her chin.

"Tell it to the judge," he said with a smirk.

Her heart sank. Was he as much a cop as Nikita had been a pregnant housekeeper? Or, as Eric had warned her, maybe he really was a cop, just a dirty one. Either way, if any of the neighbors had seen him go into her house, they wouldn't call the police. Because as far as they were concerned, he was the police.

Milan tried to formulate a plan. But just like the safe, she came up empty.

These must be the people who had killed her parents. The ones her mother and Eric had warned her against. And while Milan had a gun of her own, it was in the backpack looped over both of her shoulders. There was no point in screaming. Even if the sound made it upstairs, the windows were triple paned.

"Where is it?" Nikita said. She had a smoker's voice, low and raspy.

Anger lengthened Milan's spine, made her hands clench into fists. "Where is what?"

"The information your mother had." Nikita regarded her with narrowed eyes. "Don't play stupid."

"You absolutely do *not* have the right to remain silent," Bad Cop added.

There was no point in lying. "I don't know where it is. There's nothing like that in the safe."

"Who told you there was?" Nikita asked.

"My mom. Before she died. She said there was evidence. But there's nothing. Maybe someone else got to it first." Milan's knees went weak when she realized something. Neither Nikita nor Bad Cop was wearing a mask or anything. They didn't care if she saw their faces.

They must think she was never going to be able to tell anyone.

"You double-check," Nikita told Bad Cop. "Milan, take two steps toward me and keep your hands where I can see them."

After slipping the gun into his holster, Bad Cop moved to the workbench and started shuffling through the papers and photos, and then looking inside the envelopes to see if something had been taped there.

But he didn't have any better luck. Finally, he turned back and spread his empty hands wide. Then he leered at her. "Maybe the kid slipped something inside her bra when she had her back to you. Might be time for a strip search."

"She didn't," Nikita said flatly. She addressed her next words to Milan. "Tell me *exactly* what your mom said."

"She just gave me the key to the safe and said the evidence was inside." As she spoke, a thought nagged at Milan.

Someone at the scene of her dad's accident had put his belt around Milan's thigh as a tourniquet. She hadn't thought about that since her mom had told her in the hospital. Why? Why hadn't they let her die?

A flicker of emotion must have shown on Milan's face, because Bad Cop said, "She knows more than she's saying. Maybe she just needs some encouragement to talk." Without warning, he slapped her face.

Milan cried out, both from surprise and pain.

"Good thing none of your neighbors are close." Bad Cop was watching her avidly, as if her emotions were food for him. "You can make as much noise as you want. Or should I say, as I want." Grabbing her left hand, he smirked at her tattoo. "*What Would Jesus Do?* I think right now he would tell you to pray." Then he squeezed her fingers, grinding the broken ends of the bone together.

And then Milan did scream.

Through the tears blurring her vision, Milan saw Nikita toss an annoyed look at her torturer. "There's no need for that. I'm sure she'll see reason."

Her thoughts scurried about like a mouse caught in a maze. Could she claim the information was hidden someplace else? Once outside, she could try to break away, or at least make enough noise to draw a neighbor's attention.

But these two would ask why she hadn't gone there first.

Past Bad Cop's shoulder, Milan saw a flash of movement. A man starting to creep down the stairs, a gun in his hands and his finger on his lips.

Eric.

# Chapter 53

# JANIE

# A LONG LOOK

**Two years earlier**

KNOWING BECCA WOULD PROBABLY ARGUE AGAINST IT, JANIE COR-nered Thad in the laundry room. "I just need a little sample of the fracking fluid." Thad ran the pumper truck that injected the mix of sand, water, and chemicals in the well. Janie hadn't told Becca and Thad about meeting with Floyd, but she had started insisting they drink the water she bought. "Just something small you can put in your pocket and no one ever need know."

"What are you going to do with it?" His pale blue eyes narrowed. Normally, he called her Mom, but not now.

"I'm hoping the vet can help me figure out what's

wrong with the cows." They'd lost two more calves and another cow.

"I don't know." He looked out the window at the rain guttering down. "You know Prospect said it's not from the drilling."

There had been a spill on the well pad, but Prospect Power had said they'd cleaned it all up. After a lot of nagging, they'd sent out a veterinarian who claimed all the deaths were the result of a hodgepodge of causes: malnutrition, pink eye, copper deficiency, and fescue poisoning.

It had been insulting. Janie had been working with cows for over forty years. She knew how to take care of them.

"I don't want to just have to take their word for it. All I want to know is what's in it." Janie played her trump card. "And what about Noelle's rash?" The doctor had said the itchy rash that now ran up Noelle's torso and forearms was eczema, and asked if they had switched soaps, shampoos, or detergents. Which they hadn't.

Thad gave her a long look but ultimately agreed.

He also warned her it might take some time.

# Chapter 54

## MILAN
# WE'VE GOT NOTHING

MILAN FROZE AND THEN TORE HER GAZE AWAY FROM ERIC, WHO was standing at the top of the basement stairs. She couldn't give away his presence. She forced herself to refocus on Bad Cop while still watching Eric with her peripheral vision.

Eric's gun was aimed at the back of the other man's head. Then he waved the stubby barrel twice, silently telling Milan to get out of the line of fire.

Praying her expression hadn't betrayed his presence, Milan took a diagonal step back, as if trying to avoid having her broken finger twisted again.

*BANG!* The shot was deafening, echoing off the concrete walls of the basement. Bad Cop took a half step forward before his legs gave out. He sprawled on his belly in front of the workbench.

Nikita shouted "No!" and grabbed for Milan. Milan yanked her arm back and ran toward the stairs.

Eric was now standing on the bottom step. He pivoted, his arms held straight out in front of him, and fired two more times. He flinched each time, but still his expression was grimly determined.

Milan didn't want to look at the result, but she did anyway. Nikita clutched her chest. Her mouth and eyes went wide with surprise. She took one slow step backward and then another. Her legs gave out. She sat heavily on her butt and then slowly toppled over.

"Hurry!" Eric shouted, holding out his free hand to Milan. "Let's get out of here!"

Milan darted to the base of the stairs. Eric's hand clamped on her wrist, and then he was hauling her up behind him. When they reached the landing, he dropped her wrist so he could fling open the back door. He sprinted down the long driveway, Milan on his heels. Eric raced toward a bland blue four-door sedan parked on the street. He threw open the driver's-side door. By the time she was scrambling into the passenger seat, Eric had already started the car. When she reached for the seat belt, the gun hidden in her backpack dug painfully into her spine.

The gun. She didn't think she could have done what Eric just did.

Only after they pulled away from the curb did Milan start to cry. It was over and she was finally safe.

"Are you okay, honey?" Eric asked, his eyes on the rearview mirror. He blindly patted her knee as he pressed his foot on the accelerator.

The "honey" almost broke her. In a way, it was like having one of her parents back with her. Eric had been a part of her life for as long as she could remember.

"I think so." Milan's voice shook. "I mean, my finger's broken, but other than that—"

"That cop broke your finger?" His voice rose.

She looked down at her hands, glad that the darkness meant she couldn't see how much worse her finger was now. "He just twisted it. It got broken in the plane crash." She shivered. "Do you think he really is a cop? I mean, was?" It was still a shock to realize that the past tense was the correct one. Eric had just killed that guy.

Gritting his teeth, Eric gave his head a little shake. "I don't know if he was a cop or not. If he was, he was a dirty cop. Cops don't torture girls." Now that they were a few blocks from her house, he had slowed down to the speed limit.

Eric could go to prison for murdering Bad Cop to protect her. That is, if they lived long enough for that to happen.

Adrenaline kept coursing through Milan in waves, leaving her spent and shaking. "You just killed two people to save me."

"I'm sorry you had to see that. In fact, I'm sorry you've had to go through everything you have." Eric's voice cracked. "You have no idea how sorry I am, Milan. But I didn't have any choice. I just didn't. I did what had to be done. Sometimes you have to do things that you don't want to. That are maybe even wrong." He heaved a sigh. "What did they want?"

"They wanted to know what my mom told me before she died." Thinking of her mom's death made it hard to breathe.

His voice got softer. "Did your mom tell you what really happened to your dad? About how she figured out that Jack's accident wasn't really an accident?"

"Yeah." Milan's voice broke. "I just wish I had known that back then. I've spent months thinking it was because we were arguing and I distracted him. I thought it was all my fault that he was dead."

"Oh, honey." Eric's voice was rough. "Even your mom didn't know the truth for months. Nobody knew."

"She said Dad was killed because he had some information that people wanted to stay a secret. And then she recently found it?"

"Yeah, she told me she found a thumb drive in Jack's things. We were trying to figure out what to do with the information on it. Who to trust. I asked a buddy of mine in the FBI for advice. Only I guess he's not the stand-up guy I thought he was. Or maybe they got to him, too." Eric's words were halting. "All I know is that after I went to him, the plane blew up. And if it hadn't been for some bad sushi, I would have been on board, too."

"What *is* this information, anyway?" Milan turned in her seat. "What is so bad they were willing to kill all these people to keep it a secret?"

"It's about water pollution."

A sound that was almost a laugh was torn from her throat. The answer seemed so trivial. "*Water pollution? That's worth killing people over?*"

"It might be, if the water pollution's also killing people. If it's going to cost billions, or even trillions, to clean it up." Eric gave his head a little shake, as if clearing his thoughts. "So then after your mom talked to you, she gave you the thumb drive?"

"Mom was dying." Milan had to swallow before she could continue. "She could hardly talk. She said something about it being in the safe, but I couldn't find anything in there. And neither could those two people you shot."

He twisted his head to look at her. "It's okay, Milan. You can tell me the truth. I need to know exactly where that thumb drive is so that I can help you."

Everyone kept wanting something she didn't have. "I don't know. I looked in the safe but I couldn't find anything." Mentally, Milan again reviewed the safe's contents. Had there been a spot that could have hidden a thumb drive? Should she have pried up the black velvet lining of the jewelry boxes, felt in the dark recesses of the safe itself? "My mom said I shouldn't trust anyone and I should give the information to Mr. Kirkby. I think that's why she was coming to Portland, to talk about it with him."

"Brent, huh?" Eric said, sounding surprised. "Have you been in touch with him?"

She shook her head. "I didn't know how to do that without alerting people that I was still alive."

"What else did your mom say?"

"There wasn't anything else."

"She had to have said something more, Milan. Some clue. Something!" Eric pounded the steering wheel in frustration.

"The only other thing she said was that she loved me." Milan swallowed back a sob.

"Come on, Milan, I need you to think. That thumb drive is the key. We can't go any further without it. We need it for a bargaining chip. Without it, we've got nothing. Without it, we're dead."

"I've told you everything she said. I swear."

"I'm sorry," Eric said, "but that's not enough."

And then he made a U-turn.

# Chapter 55

## MILAN
# FUMBLED

"WHAT ARE YOU DOING?" MILAN'S HEART STUTTER-STEPPED. "You're going the wrong way."

Eric didn't answer. He just kept driving, staring straight ahead. Driving back in the direction they had just come from.

Her mom had told her to trust Brent Kirkby and no one else. Milan had thought she'd been so busy dying she'd forgotten that Eric hadn't been on the plane when the bomb went off. After all, she hadn't asked what happened to Jenna or Mark.

But maybe her mom had had other reasons for not telling her to rely on Eric.

"Where are we going?" Milan asked, unable to keep the fear from her voice. Her stomach dropped because she knew exactly where Eric was going. Back to her house. Back to the two bodies in the basement. Back to the safe he was certain held all the secrets.

Eric didn't answer.

"No, please, you can't take me back there. I searched the safe. So did that cop guy. There was nothing there. I swear it."

"Look, Milan, I'm really sorry, but I need that thumb drive. It's gotten so many people killed—but if I can get my hands on it, I'll be able to stay alive. And I want to live, Milan." His voice cracked. "You of all people should understand that."

"I understand it better than you do," she said, tears thickening her voice. "Do you know how many dead people I've seen recently? My parents. Jenna. Mark. That pilot guy, Maury." She took a deep breath. "And now those people who were waiting for me." Tears slipped from her eyes and trickled down her cheeks. "Please, I'm begging you. I can't go back in there. I can't stand seeing any more dead people."

"We just have to stay long enough to find the thumb drive." He parked in front of the house, then pulled something from his waistband and put it on his lap.

The gun. She hadn't looked at it closely in the basement. It looked old-fashioned, with a wooden handle, a short stubby barrel, and a round section that must have been for the bullets.

Panic clutched at her throat. Why did he still need the

gun? Did he think Nikita and Bad Cop might not be all the way dead? "Then let me stay in the car," she pleaded. In her mind's eye she kept seeing an endless awful rotation of images: Maury's headless body, Mark's empty eyes, Jenna's blood-painted face, her mom taking her last breath. Milan couldn't bear to see any more.

"Your mom told only one person where it is. You. I need you with me. I swear it will be okay." Eric reached over and squeezed her shoulder, his voice a little less soothing. "Just keep trying to think of where your mom might have hidden it." He picked up the gun and got out of the car.

Eric actually thought Milan was holding back. She could see it. "I honestly don't know. I swear it!"

They moved silently down the driveway. The back door was still unlocked. With the gun, Eric motioned for Milan to go ahead of him. She was breathing shallowly, not wanting to smell the coppery scent of blood. As she started down the stairs, she kept her head up, resolutely not looking down at the bodies.

But when she finally checked, halfway down, she froze. The woman and the man weren't dead. They didn't even seem injured. Instead they were on their feet, looking up the stairs expectantly.

A wave of dizziness passed over her. She swayed and had to steady herself on the wall. Her head felt like an untethered balloon.

"Eric?" Milan turned. "They're not dead."

"I'm sorry, honey." He didn't meet her eyes. "I owed some really bad guys a lot of money. They were going to kill me. These people offered me a way out."

Horror closed her throat. Eric was working with them. Just like he had told her in the car, he wanted to live. And he was willing to pay any price. Including other people's lives.

Even hers.

"What about the gun?" she managed to choke out. "I saw you shoot them."

"Starter pistol. It just shoots blanks."

"Acting!" Bad Cop threw out his free hand dramatically. His other hand still held his gun. "Don't worry. Ours are real."

"Did you get her to talk?" Nikita asked.

"I tried, but she's still insisting she doesn't know anything," Eric said. He looked at Nikita. "I did everything you asked. That has to count for something."

Bad Cop grunted and threw a disgusted look at Nikita. "I told you we shouldn't have been soft on her."

"But I really don't know anything." Milan's voice was shaking, and she didn't try to control it. She *was* scared. She was exhausted. There was no way she could get to the gun in the backpack, not in time. But still, she had two advantages. One was that they probably wouldn't want to kill her immediately, not when they still thought she might lead them to the thumb drive. The other was that she knew this space, knew it as well as she knew any other room in

237

her house. She had been left down here countless times in the dark. Her mom had always been hypervigilant about snapping off lights she thought weren't being used.

Milan launched herself down the last few steps and across the floor, Eric on her heels.

She flung open the door to the electrical panel. With both hands, she flipped all the circuit breakers.

The basement was plunged into darkness. Eric let out a shout. As she yanked her dad's key ring from the safe, someone jostled her, but Milan managed to stay on her feet. Hands grabbed for her. She pivoted, pulling out of their grasp as she slid the keys into her pocket. She darted, not toward the stairs, but farther into the basement. Her outstretched hand found what she was looking for.

The rack of croquet mallets. After grabbing one, she cut back toward the stairs. When her foot found the first step, she started up. But instead of facing up as she climbed, Milan turned to face the basement. When a hand grabbed her ankle, she blindly swung the mallet. A man grunted as it connected. With his head, Milan guessed. Hoped.

Finally, her butt bumped the door. She was at the top. Stepping back into the entryway, she slammed the door closed. Her fingers fumbled as she tried to shut the bolt.

*Hurry*, Milan screamed silently to herself as footsteps pounded up the stairs. *Hurry!* Finally the bolt slid into place.

And then she was flinging open the back door and racing out.

# Chapter 56

MILAN

# MAKE A NOISE

IN THE DARK, MILAN SPRINTED THROUGH THE BACK DOOR, NOT even pausing to close it. She ran around the corner of the house toward the Prius, her right hand already outstretched, clicking the fob. But ahead of her was no answering chirp, no flash of lights. She figured that the fob's battery must be dead.

After sliding her fingers down to the keys, she plucked out one. But when she tried to put it in the lock, her hand shook so hard the key just scratched around the keyhole for several long seconds. *Come on, come on*, Milan muttered to herself, before the tip finally caught.

Her relief lasted less than a nanosecond. The key refused to go in any farther.

She was running out of time. In her mind's eye, Milan kept picturing the sliding bolt now holding the basement door closed. It was a flimsy thing, the metal thinner than a pencil. It had mostly been intended to keep Frank, their elderly, half-blind dog—gone six years now—from nosing open the door and tumbling down the stairs. Certainly it hadn't been designed to prevent an able-bodied adult from shouldering the door open. Eventually the flimsy metal would bend, or the shallow screws pull right out of the frame.

Or maybe they would just shoot it.

And then they would come careening around the corner and find her. Helpless, alone, out in the open. Too focused on getting in the car to realize she had to run.

As Milan tried to select a second key, the ring slipped from her fingers and jangled to the ground. When she leaned down to retrieve it, dizziness engulfed her, forcing her to take a half step forward. Her head bumped painfully against the door. She ignored it all, focused on getting away.

Snatching up the key ring, she plucked out a key and tried again to jam it into the lock, not knowing if it was a new key or the same one she'd already tried. Whatever it was, it also refused to go in more than a third of an inch. By now, Milan's shoulders were up around her ears as she imagined a bullet striking her in the back.

In the darkness, she held up the key ring and squinted

at the half dozen keys. None looked right. The killers would be out here any second. She needed to abandon the car and start running, but where? Whatever Milan did, she had to be quick.

She needed to run. Now. Had to.

Didn't she?

Milan made a decision.

Instead of sprinting down the street, she turned around, then scurried back the way she had come, going back into the house through the open door. The basement door was still closed, but it was creaking from the rhythmic thumps of someone trying to force it open.

Milan slipped past. Thankful for the silent rubber soles of her Doc Martens, she ran on tiptoe through the tiled kitchen and down the hall. Working on muscle memory, she deftly avoided the one spot of the floor that always squeaked.

In the living room, she flipped open the two locks on the front door in case she had to leave. Then she opened the coat closet. Her heart lurched when the door let out a soft creak. But at the same time, the door from the basement crashed open, drowning out the noise she had made.

Milan slipped inside the closet, pushing past the coats, and held her breath as she slowly, carefully pulled the door closed.

This time it didn't make a noise.

On the other side of the house Milan heard the killers

run out through the door she had left open. The woman's low voice issued terse commands to the others. Including Eric. Eric, who knew this house as well as Milan did.

Eric, who had betrayed her. Who must have known about the bomb on the plane, or else why would he have not boarded? Eric, who had let Jenna and Mark and the pilot die. Who had let her mother die.

Who had decided that when it came right down to it, all that mattered was that *he* didn't die.

Milan closed her eyes, not that it made any difference in the darkness, and leaned her head against the wall.

# Chapter 57

# JANIE
# CLEARLY NOTHING

**Two years earlier**

JANIE DECIDED TO KEEP HER DAIRY OPERATION GOING, DESPITE the dead cows, despite the lower milk yield, despite the fact there were now twenty-two shale-gas wells within a five-mile radius of her farm. What else was she going to do?

Two days ago, Thad had slipped her a small bottle of fracking fluid, not meeting her eyes. Today, she was going to give it to Floyd.

As she walked out to her truck, she heard a strange buzzing noise and went into the field.

Another dead cow. Janie's heart lurched, even as she pulled out her cell phone and filmed what she saw with a shaking hand. The dead cow was engulfed in a black, humming mist. She zoomed in. Hundreds of flies. Maybe thousands.

Janie backed away, mouth closed, trying not to breathe. She would have to bury it this afternoon, next to the others. But first she would give Floyd the fracking fluid and this video and the others she had made. One of them showed the creek, where the water used to be so clear you could see every pebble on the bottom. Now it ran dirty brown, with sudsy bubbles wherever it pushed past rocks.

They met at the playground again, even though this time she didn't have the grandkids with her.

"I tested your water," Floyd said as he tucked the small vial of fracking fluid into his pocket. "I found a type of PFAS at .35 parts per billion."

Janie's shoulders relaxed. One third of a part per billion? That was clearly nothing. But he was still speaking.

"The EPA's new limit is four parts per quadrillion."

Billions Janie could sort of think about. Maybe trillions. Wasn't a quadrillion some kind of ballroom dance they did in the nineteenth century? It certainly didn't seem like something a regular person could understand.

He must have seen her expression. "Four parts per quadrillion is vanishingly small. It's the same as one second compared to eight million years." That sounded bad, but his next words were a gut punch. "What's in your water is more than eighty-seven thousand times that. The level is so high I'm guessing there must have been a casing failure in your wellbore or maybe in one of your neighbors'. Something's releasing fracking fluid into the underground aquifer. Whatever the source, you shouldn't be drinking it. You shouldn't brush your teeth with it. You shouldn't even shower in it. Because some of it is going to aerosolize and you're going to breathe it in."

He kept saying "you," but it wasn't just her. It was her daughter. Thad. Her grandkids. Including the one who hadn't even been born yet. Suddenly Janie found herself on her knees, dry heaving.

Floyd helped her to her feet. And when Janie got up, she vowed to fight.

# Chapter 58

## MILAN
# A SAFE PLACE

MILAN HELD HER BREATH, STRAINING TO LISTEN FROM INSIDE THE closet. The neighborhood was quiet enough that she could hear one car start up and then another. But had all three people left—or only two?

Slowly, she eased open the door to the closet and slipped out, gently closing it behind her. She repeated the process with the front door.

As she started down the stairs, a bright light suddenly illuminated her from behind. A scream leaped into her throat and lodged there. She jumped the last two steps. The impact jarred up the length of her body, but Milan kept moving, turning to face whoever was holding the flashlight. But no one was on the porch. The light was coming from the outside light that automatically came on when it detected movement.

Had it alerted anyone? Milan heard no shouts or running feet. She kept picturing their faces. Nikita expressionless in the motel room. Bad Cop grinning as he twisted her broken finger. Eric apologizing before handing her back over to them.

How long did she have to find a safe place to hide? Milan cut through her yard, the grass muffling her footfalls, using the bushes and trees for cover. The clouds had thinned. From overhead a few stars gazed down, cold and impersonal.

Across the street, the lights in both the Diazes' living room and Chance's bedroom were on. If she went up to their front door and knocked, how would his parents react? They would probably want to do what parents always thought was a good idea—call the police. If they had watched the news, maybe they would even refuse to let her in.

But Chance would believe her. Right? Even if he just let her hide in his room for a couple of hours, it would give her a moment to rest. An opportunity to lose her pursuers. And time to figure out what to do next.

Milan watched the street for a long time before daring to dart across it. When she did, she was as swift as an arrow released from a bow. In a few seconds, she was standing on the soft bed of bark dust under Chance's window, sweat tracing her spine.

After lifting her hand to tap on the glass, Milan hesitated. Was it fair to drag him into her new upside-down world? One where motel maids were assassins, and men dressed like cops twisted your broken bones, and someone you would have trusted with your life betrayed you?

Maybe, even without the thumb drive, she should just go to Mr. Kirkby. She suddenly remembered that in the car, back when she thought she could trust Eric, she had told him about Mr. Kirkby. Maybe they were heading there, hoping to find her.

There were no good answers. So Milan tapped her fingertips lightly on the glass.

The blinds stayed where they were. No sounds came from Chance's room—no music or TV. Maybe he was listening with earbuds in. Or maybe he wasn't in his room at all.

Then suddenly the blinds were being pushed aside as Chance ducked under them. Even in silhouette, she knew every line of him. The window slid open. "Milan?" Chance said softly. "What are you doing here?" His voice held an unfamiliar note of caution.

"I—I'm sorry. I don't know what I was thinking. Forget I was ever here." Milan started to back away.

"Wait!" His whisper was urgent.

She hesitated. "Maybe I shouldn't have come here. It's not safe to be around me. People are trying to kill me. Only—only I don't know where else to go."

For an answer, he leaned down and offered his hands.

After a moment's hesitation, Milan grabbed with just her right, whispering to him that her other hand had a broken finger. His fingers, cool and slightly calloused, wrapped around her left wrist. When he pulled her up, she smelled his familiar smell, a mixture of soap and spice. Between him pulling and her scrabbling her feet up the lapped exterior boards, she managed to get her hips past the sill. There wasn't room to throw a leg over, so she tugged her hands free from Chance's, put them on the floor, and walked them forward until the rest of her body slid down like a snake.

Was she a snake? Had she just brought all her troubles to her oldest friend?

Chance put his finger to his lips as he reached down with his other hand to help her up. He put his mouth close to her ear.

"I'm guessing you don't want my parents to know you're here."

She shook her head. "I'm scared, Chance," she whispered back. "Somebody bombed my mom's plane and now they're hunting me. I don't know what to do." Her whisper got breathier and more wobbly. "I need a safe place to hide for a while and think, and I was hoping—"

Milan didn't have to finish her thought, because Chance was hugging her and whispering, "Of course you can stay here."

# Chapter 59

LENNY

# CLEAN UP THIS MESS

LENNY SLAMMED HER HAND ON THE SUBARU'S STEERING WHEEL SO hard it hurt her palm. It was weak to show emotion, but she was alone in the car, having ordered Roscoe to go with Eric. She didn't trust either of them, but they also didn't trust each other. Maybe if she was lucky, they would shoot each other.

As she drove up and down the empty streets looking for Milan, she considered Eric. He had always been the weak point. Lenny had been working with, or more accurately *on*, him for months, not long after Jack started nosing around. It was clear Jack had received information from someone with knowledge about Prospect Power.

After taking care of Floyd Higgins, she'd worked to plug the leak. She'd probed for Jack's weak spots and found none. So she'd widened the net.

Eric had gambling debts. In return for the promise of paying them off, he'd tried to find the information. But his clumsy searching—leaving footprints on a freshly vacuumed carpet, leaving the blinds at a different angle—had made Jack even more cautious. The best Eric had managed was to figure out that it was a thumb drive, and that Jack always carried it on his person.

But after causing Jack's fatal car accident, Lenny had found nothing in his wallet, pockets, or bag. The client had been disappointed, but when the questions stopped, it had seemed that they were in the clear.

But then, months after her husband's death, Heather started making discreet inquiries. It was clear the thumb drive had somehow turned up again.

A bomb had seemed the best solution. Take out Heather and her inner circle, including Eric. Silence anyone who might know just what Floyd had sent. Lenny had stuck to the plan, even when she learned Milan would be on board the plane.

It was just Lenny's bad luck that Eric had spotted the bomb. But once the news reported Milan was alive, he had wisely decided to try to get back on Lenny's good side.

He had said that if they couldn't force Milan to hand

over the information, he would be able to get her to do it willingly if she thought he was still on her side. He'd assured Lenny that Milan thought of him as practically another parent. That she would trust him.

Only Milan didn't and hadn't. Even the charade with the starter pistol Lenny had given Eric hadn't loosened her tongue.

Now it seemed likely he would go rabbiting off again. Maybe even try to cut a deal with the feds.

Eric had outlived his usefulness.

But if Lenny didn't clean up this mess, the client might decide she had outlived hers. Her guess was that he had hired Roscoe to clean up the loose ends that both she and Milan represented.

Keeping exactly to the speed limit, Lenny drove in a grid pattern, her head swiveling from side to side, looking for movement. She already knew she wouldn't spot Milan running in a blind panic. On foot, the girl could slide into shadows, hide behind a tree, bush, or building, as she must have in Bend.

Milan had known exactly how to use her home turf for maximum advantage. And she'd refused to admit what she knew, even to someone she should have trusted. Even when Roscoe was hurting her. Although maybe by staying silent she had revealed too much. A civilian would have made up a lie, said whatever they needed to get the pain to stop.

The girl must have been taught how to manage pain. It explained how she had managed to survive so far. Pain would not motivate her, just as it wouldn't Lenny. Milan would be able to withstand increasing trauma until her body went into shock or her mind flew away.

So maybe the way for Lenny to find Milan was to think like her. And what would Lenny do in this situation?

First of all, she would not consider herself a victim. Do that and you were lost. Instead Milan must be planning how to turn the tables. She was clearly not afraid to get her hands dirty, or to hurt someone. Lenny realized she was unconsciously rubbing the bruises left by the motel phone's handset.

She turned onto a new street. In the last fifteen minutes, she had passed only one other car. The roads here were wide and quiet. Even at night, it was clear how green and verdant everything was.

How many hours had she spent driving next to her dad on nights like this? Or just sitting on a stakeout while he held a pair of binoculars or a camera? Every seven or eight minutes, Karl would hold up two fingers on his right hand, the signal for Lenny to light a cigarette and pass it to him.

Lenny felt a tickle, and then the cough was back. It was a long time before she could stop. Her chest ached.

What would Karl say if he were here? A lot. He would say Lenny had gotten complacent. That she liked making things too complicated. That she had let sentimentality get the best of her. That Milan was a weak point.

So what were Milan's weak points? Lenny thought about Brent Kirkby. Milan's mom had told her to go to him once she had the thumb drive. Wheels within wheels, layers upon layers.

# Chapter 60

## MILAN
# THE SAME QUESTION

CHANCE TOOK MILAN'S GOOD HAND AND TUGGED. TOGETHER, THEY sat on the edge of his bed. The blue cotton bedspread was new, but otherwise everything—the crowded book-shelves, the orange beanbag in the far corner, the posters on the wall—was as familiar as her own room. But Milan no longer felt like a teenager.

"So is it true?" Chance whispered. "You were in a plane crash? Your mom's dead?"

So much had happened in the last two days—was it only two days?—that it was hard to know where to start. But Milan did her best, often having to loop back to explain something she had skipped. At one point, Chance left to get her a glass of water and to preemptively say good night to his parents. When he returned, he turned off the light so they would think he was asleep. Milan whispered to him in the dark.

After his parents had gone to bed themselves, he ventured out again. When he returned, he had a roll of medical tape and a plate of food, and he turned the light back on.

"Your finger really needs to be looked at by a doctor," he said. "I mean, I learned some basics in Boy Scouts, but this is your hand, and hands are important."

Before all this happened, the sight of her left ring finger, swollen and purple like some kind of diseased slug, would have reduced Milan to tears. Now she shrugged. "I have nine more. I'm just glad I'm right-handed."

Chance had her wash down two Advil with the glass of milk he'd brought. Then he knelt in front of her and set about buddy taping her ring finger to her pinkie while she took a bite of the almond butter and strawberry jam sandwich he had made her.

"Shouldn't you tape it to my middle finger?" she asked as he wound the tape around.

"This will make it easier to grip things." Because Milan's pinkie finger was so much shorter, Chance had to angle the tape. The first time wasn't quite right, so he was forced to pull it off and start over.

Milan didn't flinch. She just kept eating. In addition to the sandwich, there was a Honeycrisp apple that lived up to its name. Chance was committed to healthy food, but she was beginning to think there wasn't much point. If you were going to die soon, why not gorge on Doritos and Ben & Jerry's?

Still, it tasted amazing. She polished off the last few bites while she finished catching him up on the condensed version of what had happened.

"So where *is* this thumb drive they all want?" His dark brows drew together.

Everyone always had the same question, and Milan never had an answer. "That's the problem. I don't know." She set the plate and glass on his desk, then wiped her mouth with the paper towel he had thoughtfully provided. Against its pristine white, her scratched and battered hands looked like they belonged to some kind of monster.

"That sucks." He ran his fingers through his thick straight hair, leaving it in little black spikes. "And the information is about water pollution?"

"Yeah, and if Eric's telling the truth, it's killing people, and will cost billions to clean up." A wave of exhaustion crested over her. She flopped back on the bed and then scooted up, grabbed one of his two pillows, and fitted it behind her head.

Chance stretched out next to her.

"I don't know where it is any more than they do. I don't think it's in the safe. I looked at everything, and then they did, too. Maybe someone else already took it."

"Tell me again what your mom said," Chance asked. "The exact words."

Milan took a deep, hitching breath. Every time she thought about her mom, it was like pressing a bruise over and over to see if it still hurt. Or worse than that. It was like sticking your fingers in a wound to see if it was still bleeding. "She told me to be careful. She said something about the proof and the safe."

"Wait a minute," Chance said. Their faces were only inches apart. "Did she say *the* safe? Or was she telling you to *be* safe?"

"I don't know." Her words trailed off. "I'm positive she said the evidence was inside."

"But inside what?"

The more Milan tried to remember her mom's exact words, the more they slipped away. "It definitely had to do with the keys." She propped herself on one elbow. "Maybe Mom meant it was inside the house or even the car." But if it was, how would they find it? How long would it take to search every inch of a two-thousand-square-foot house, especially if you didn't know what you were looking for?

Chance unfolded the quilt at the end of his bed and spread it over her. "Maybe you should try to get some sleep. Things might seem clearer in the morning."

Technically it was already morning. The alarm clock next to his bed said it was just after midnight.

"I don't think anything's going to seem clearer ever." But still Milan put her head down and closed her eyes.

# Chapter 61

MILAN

# SOME PEOPLE ARE SAYING

MILAN WOKE TO A HAND OVER HER MOUTH AND SIRENS CUTTING through the night. She bucked and twisted until she figured out the hand belonged to Chance. He was trying to keep her from giving herself away to his parents.

After she stilled, they both got up and went to the window, Milan moving as stiffly as an eighty-year-old. Chase turned a slat so they could peek through. One police car in front of her house and another in her driveway, behind the Prius. Both with their red-and-blue lights twirling.

It was later than she had first thought. The sun was just starting to come up. A few neighbors were gathering outside wearing bathrobes or coats, a couple with cups of coffee.

Was there any chance they could see her? She stepped back.

Chance whispered, "I'll go head my parents off before they come in here. But just to be safe, you should probably hide in my closet. I'll report back."

Chance's closet smelled like him. Milan sat on the bumpy tops of his shoes, too tired to pile them to one side and clear a space. His shirts hung around her, gently brushing her shoulders and the top of her head. She was tired of hiding, of finding refuge only to have it snatched away. Her heart was a piece of paper the universe kept crumpling, smoothing out, and then crumpling again.

She didn't mean to, but she must have slept, her forehead resting against her bent knees. When Chance opened the closet door, she jolted upright.

He squatted in front of her. "Okay, the medical examiner's van just left. They took away two body bags."

She closed her eyes for a long moment. "One of them has to be Eric." It seemed clear he had been alive only because he offered access to what she supposedly possessed. And once that didn't pan out, what did they need him for? "They must have come back when they couldn't find me."

The other dead person had to be Bad Cop or Nikita. Bad Cop had seemed willing to do anything, but Nikita was like a precision-guided missile.

"All the neighbors seem to think someone decided to

burglarize your house after hearing about the plane crash. Mrs. Littlefield talked to a cop who said the whole place was torn up, like they were looking for valuables."

Which they had been. Not jewelry, cash, gold, or guns. But information. Information that had so far led to—Milan counted on her fingers—seven people being killed.

"So do the neighbors have any guesses as to why there were two dead people at my house?" Dead for real this time.

"The most popular theory seems to be they must have found something really good and had an argument over who got to keep it." He looked at her. "Do you think it's possible they did find the thumb drive?"

She shrugged. "Maybe." The thought brought an odd kind of relief.

He cleared his throat. "There's another theory, though."

"What?" She already had some idea.

"Some people are saying you might have done it."

"Why would I tear up my own house and then kill two people?"

He wrinkled his nose. "That's why no one really believes it."

But his face said that maybe some people did.

Chapter 62

MILAN
# FLED THE SCENE

LATE LAST NIGHT, CHANCE HAD SNUCK MILAN NEXT DOOR TO HIS
bathroom. She had used it as quickly as possible in the
dark, every nerve alert for the sound of one of his parents
deciding to pad down the hall for a midnight snack.

Now that his parents had gone to work, she took a little
more time. She washed her face, her right hand, and the
unbandaged part of her left. She raised her eyes to look at
her reflection. Even though the person in the mirror still
looked so different, with short hair and shadowed eyes,
this new face was starting to seem more familiar. There
was no softness in it.

As Milan dried her hands, her eyes focused on her tattoo. WWJD? What would her dad tell her to do in this

situation? Maybe he would tell her to walk away, to go as far as she could get and never look back.

No. Her dad would never say that. He always said you stood up for what you believed in.

Back in Chance's room, Milan sat down at his desktop computer. He was in the kitchen, making breakfast.

CNN had a story labeled "Breaking News."

---

## TWO BODIES FOUND IN SENATOR MAYHEW'S HOME

This morning, the bodies of two men were found in Oregon senator Heather Mayhew's Portland residence. Authorities said both had gunshot wounds, but they were otherwise tight-lipped about who the victims were or any evidence police have found.

After the plane crash earlier this week that resulted in the deaths of Senator Mayhew and three other people on board, the senator's sixteen-year-old daughter, Milan Mayhew, is still missing. Ten months ago, Milan was also the only survivor of a car accident that killed her father, the late senator Jack Mayhew.

Authorities would not address rumors that Milan Mayhew fled the scene of the plane crash before the wreckage was discovered.

She clicked on other news sites, but they all had the same information, which they treated in different ways. On some, she was Miss Mayhew, and they didn't try to draw lines between her and all the bad things that had happened. On more than a few, she had already been tried and found guilty.

Milan jumped when Chance opened the bedroom door. "Breakfast is ready."

She followed him out to the kitchen. Toast, orange juice, coffee, scrambled eggs. It was pretty much what she had fantasized about while lost in the woods. Only, she had imagined that she would feel safe when she ate them. She thanked him as she picked up her fork.

"Right now, there's only one cop car left in front of the house. After they leave, we can get your mom's car and go to Mr. Kirkby."

She pulled the key ring from her pocket. Now that she was no longer in a panic, it was clear one of the keys did belong to a car.

"The fob is out of juice. I just hope the car isn't. It's not like we can call Triple A for a jump."

"I wonder what kind of batteries it takes. Maybe one of those that looks like a coin? My parents have some like that, but I don't know if they're the right size."

He went down into the basement and came back with a tiny screwdriver and an old shoebox full of different-sized batteries. There was only one battery that looked right.

"Let's hope that's the right one," he said, holding out his hand for the key ring. The tip of his tongue poked out between his lips as he tried to fit the tiny screwdriver into the corresponding slot on the fob.

After a few seconds, Milan was the one to hold out her hand. "Let me do that. My hands are smaller."

She squinted to set the blade in the slot, then gave it a few quick turns. A sense of satisfaction filled her as the lid popped off.

But inside was no flat silver circle.

Instead a black niche held a thumb drive.

# Chapter 63

JANIE

# BEFORE HE EVEN DREW A BREATH

### Nine months earlier

JANIE HAD DONE HER BEST. AFTER TALKING TO FLOYD, SHE wouldn't let anyone drink from the tap. She bought a water tank—called a buffalo—that sat in the yard like some kind of oversize gray marshmallow.

There were now a few people in the county like Janie, people who were growing disillusioned. Many of the promised jobs had lasted only as long as the wells needed to be drilled, the pipes run. But the need for construction jobs was drying up, and the day-to-day operations were run by a relatively small number of employees.

Both Darcy and Noelle had been diagnosed with asthma. Janie's friend who was a nurse at the hospital said they were starting to see people with infections that wouldn't clear without massive doses of multiple antibiotics. Her neighbor Tracy Brandies got admitted for fever and belly pain so bad it left her weeping. They found growths on her thyroid and colon. Three days after Tracy was admitted to the hospital, her spleen burst.

Becca's baby died in her womb. She was already six months along. They had to bury little Bart before he even drew a breath. And when the doctors did the autopsy, they found he didn't have a bladder or kidneys.

Two weeks later, Becca and Thad quit their jobs, packed up the kids, and moved out of the state.

And now Janie was alone, with only Rocky for company.

Only lately his breathing had sounded harsh.

# Chapter 64

## MILAN

# NO SUCH THING AS A FREE LUNCH

THIS WAS WHAT MILAN'S MOTHER HAD MEANT BY *SAFE* AND *inside*. Not inside the safe, the house, or even the car. Milan had been carrying the information all this time. Milan and her mom had shared a love for *The Wizard of Oz*, and for a second she heard the voice of Glinda the Good Witch in her head.

*You always had the power, my dear, you just had to learn it for yourself.*

Chance slid the thumb drive into the back of his computer. It took so long for anything to pop up on his screen that Milan thought the drive might be empty or damaged. But finally an icon appeared, and she double-clicked on it.

Inside were a half dozen folders. She read the labels.

Lab reports. Safety data sheets. Photos. Recordings. Medical records.

Taking the mouse, Milan clicked on the one folder she was sure she would understand. Photos. After selecting the entire list, she double-clicked to open all of them.

The smile drained from her face like water.

Labeled "Elijah Farnish," the first photo her eyes focused on was of a premature baby, red and raw-looking. Elijah was far too skinny, a cannula taped under his nose, monitors and IVs taped to his tiny feet, wrists, chest.

Behind her, Chance sucked in his breath. Milan's eyes jumped from photo to photo.

A creek filled with opaque, reddish-brown water that looked more like used motor oil.

Another stream, the water clearer, but this one was bordered with hundreds of dead fish, silver bellies to the sky.

A young girl pulling up her shirt to show an angry red rash covering her torso.

A half dozen dead spotted frogs on the muddy edge of a small pond.

A gray-haired woman standing over a blue barrel, looking at a yellow handheld monitor. Whatever she saw was making her press her turquoise-colored scarf over her nose and mouth.

Two horses, brown and black, standing with heads bowed. They looked brittle, just skin over bones.

Three dead birds, brown with white breasts, lying on

their sides among stalks of corn. Mouths open. Eyes open and dull.

A man holding up two repurposed clear plastic bottles that had once held water or soda. Now one was filled with yellow-tan liquid, and the other with milk-chocolate brown. Milan knew just by looking at his expression that both were supposed to be clear.

Four dead black-and-white cows lying on their sides, so bloated that their top legs stuck up in the air like a nightmare chorus line.

A narrow pipe as tall as the trees around it, venting a plume of yellow and orange fire billowing hundreds of feet into the sky.

The thing was, Milan had seen similar photos. The standpipe venting fire to the sky. The various shades of what had once been clean water.

"Eric said this was about water pollution," she said to Chance. "But I think it's also got something to do with fracking. Remember how I gave that report on it?"

Still staring at the photos, he lifted one shoulder. "To be honest, no."

She rolled her eyes. "You were right there!" It felt weird to tease him about something so serious, but also oddly good. "Don't you remember how I got an A after my dad basically rewrote it?"

Her dad had been passionate about the potential problems of fracking. Oregon didn't have the right kind of shale deposits for fracking, but her dad had started paying attention after it was revealed that two million pounds of radioactive fracking waste had been illegally sent to a rural Oregon dump.

It wasn't just the chemicals used to frack that could be dangerous. Water shot underground to free oil or gas also freed the naturally occurring radioactive isotopes that had been safely locked in the bedrock.

The fracking waste turned out to be 340 times more radioactive than the highest level the state allowed.

Her dad was always talking about the fracking industry's web of companies, how they deliberately made everything complicated, with layers of businesses and subsidiaries and subcontractors, trying to reduce the chance anyone would be held responsible. And like a game of telephone, accurate information got lost along the way.

Now Milan touched her tattoo. "My dad used to say all water is connected. Rain is connected to rivers are connected to streams are connected to the underground aquifers that feed the ocean that evaporates and becomes rain."

Milan clicked on an icon for a video file. Shaky cell phone camera footage of an overturned truck, fluid leaking out of it and down a hill. Another video showed a broken pipeline spewing dark liquid. The next showed a cow covered in a black moving layer of flies.

She opened more files. The medical records were listed under people's names, with a word or two for what was wrong. *Delilah Green, liver cancer. Lucas Burbank, asthma. Precious Brown, kidney cancer. Baby Cordello, miscarriage. Elijah Metcalf, premature.*

"Whatever is in the water," Chance said, "it looks like animals and even people are dying because of it."

"And other people are dying so it can be kept secret. At least six—no, seven—people have died already." Milan felt bad that she kept forgetting about the pilot. Even though she still had his gun. "Eric said cleaning it up would cost billions or even trillions of dollars."

Inside the file for lab reports were more file folders. One was for wells, each labeled with a name: Bronson's well, Kinnamen's well, Metcalf's well, Testori's well.

Another held lab reports from streams. Mad Creek, Rocky Brook, Bottle Creek, Fordyce Creek, Broken Branch River, Looking Glass Creek. Milan recognized some of the names because they had also been on the photos.

And another file held the names of towns, each followed by the words *municipal water*: Smithfield, South Lake, Tiller, Parishville, Sixmile.

As Milan read the names of the towns out loud, Chance Google-Mapped them on his phone. "Those places are all thirty, forty miles apart in the Midwest." He typed some more. "And this company called Prospect Power started fracking there about three years ago."

Milan pointed. "But look—they're doubled up. There's two for each town." Then she squinted, trying to see what was different. "They have different dates. One's for last year, and the others are all at least three years old."

The only test without two listings was labeled "Prospect Power's fracking solution."

She opened it. The lab results meant nothing to her. The names of the chemicals were mouthfuls, so long that by the time she had read all the way to the end she had forgotten what the term began with. "Nonionic fluorosurfactant," she said out loud.

"I think a surfactant is something that acts like soap," Chance said, then hesitated. "I think."

"Fluorinated carboxylic acid."

He shook his head and didn't even bother to hazard a guess.

The computer screen was wide enough that Milan could open two documents and look at them side by side. She left one for a town open and then clicked on the report for the fracking solution. Her eyes went back and forth between the two.

Chance gave voice to what she was seeing. "The same chemicals that are in Prospect Power's fracking solution are in the town's water supply."

Milan opened the older file for the same town, already knowing what she would find. "And look—four years ago, before the fracking, there weren't these chemicals."

Chance whistled. "It wouldn't be too hard to connect the dots."

In the file labeled "Recordings," Milan clicked on one labeled with a date and the words "Beau Beauford, Prospect Power plant manager."

A man said, "There's always give-and-take, Floyd. You know that. There's no such thing as a free lunch. A few fish die, a couple of birds, a horse gets sick—so what? First of all, everything dies. Everyone dies. You can try to point a finger at Prospect Power, but good luck finding anyone to take your case. In fact, you seem to be the only one who's bothered. A long time ago, your town's get-up-and-go done got up and went, but since we started drilling, it's jumping. All the restaurants and hotels and stores around here are booming. There's brand-new Ford and Chevy pickups sitting in people's driveways. They got their houses fixed up and paid off their loans. And you want to go and ruin everything just for some puny creek and a few warblers?"

The recording ended there.

The second one was just labeled "Threat from _____?" with a date a week after the first. It was a different voice but still a man's.

"Hey, Higgins, you'd better just stop what you're doing. Sticking your nose in where it don't belong. You get paid to run reports. You don't get paid to think. And you most especially don't get paid to talk."

# Chapter 65

## MILAN

# THESE PEOPLE AREN'T PLAYING

MILAN MET CHANCE'S EYES. WERE HERS AS WIDE AS HIS? "SO SOME-one must have sent this thumb drive to my dad."

He nodded, his eyes never leaving hers.

She took a deep breath. "And when he started asking questions, someone killed him."

"And eventually your mom must have found the information like we did—trying to change the battery." Chance's expression was grim. "And we know what happened next."

Milan again saw her mom's face as pale as the snow beneath her while orange flames billowed from the broken plane. "That must be why she told me to go to Brent Kirkby. He's not just my godfather. He also started Earth Energy and then hired my dad to run it."

"So do you think he can help us? Because these people aren't playing. They will do anything to keep this a secret."

A thought distracted her. "If they killed my parents, what did they do to the person who sent them the information? The first recording was that Prospect Power guy talking to someone named Floyd, right?"

Milan clicked on the second recording. "Hey, Higgins, you'd better just stop what you're doing."

After opening up a browser window, Milan typed in "Floyd Higgins." Then after thinking a second, she added the word "laboratory."

A six-month-old news story was the top result.

---

## LOCAL MAN SEVERELY INJURED IN FALL

A 54-year-old man has sustained life-threatening injuries in a fall at his home. The Parishville police department, responding to a request for a welfare check, found Floyd Higgins on the concrete basement floor of his home, according to a news release issued by the police department. It appears that Higgins survived for three days without food or water after tumbling down the stairs of his Terrace Drive home. Higgins, who is a senior water quality scientist at Alexis Analytical Laboratories, last worked on Friday. He was discovered late Tuesday morning, when

police were asked to check on him due to his failure
to report to work or respond to his son's phone calls.

Sergeant John Dominguez stated that he was surprised to still find Higgins alive, saying, "It's a miracle
he survived that fall....We could barely wake him.
The gentleman has a strong will."

Neighbors say they hadn't seen Higgins since Friday evening but thought nothing of it because he
often works long hours.

As Milan read, the hairs on the back of her neck prick-
led. Her head was throbbing. Fingers slick on the keys, she
searched for "Floyd Higgins obituary" but found only versions of the same news story.

Chance touched her wrist. "Are you sure we shouldn't
go to the police? What's this Mr. Kirkby going to do against
some cold-blooded killers? Is he like a ninja or something?
Does he have an assault rifle or a safe room?"

The questions would have been funny in any other con-
text. "He's like a grandpa. You know, white hair, the kind
of guy who wears short-sleeved dress shirts. All I know is
he's the only person my mom said I should trust. We still
don't even know if that guy in my basement was a cop."

"Speaking of cops..." Chance went to the window and
peeped through the blinds. "The squad car is gone, and most
of the people on this block work during the day. I'll see if I
can get the car started. If I can, you just run out and get in."

"And then we'll go straight to Mr. Kirkby." She reviewed the plan, such as it was, in her head. What if it all went wrong? "But maybe we can make a stop first."

"Where?"

"Merrow Cemetery. I want to visit my dad's grave."

He quirked an eyebrow until she told him why.

# Chapter 66

## MILAN
# NIGHTMARES CAN COME TRUE

MILAN HAD HURRIED TO HER MOM'S CAR WITHOUT DRAWING ANY-
one's attention. After visiting the cemetery, Chance followed Milan's directions to Mr. Kirkby's house. She felt
numb, but there was no turning back now.

Mr. Kirkby lived in a rural area outside Portland city
limits. If she had actually tried to walk here, it would have
taken hours. The farther out they drove, the bigger and
farther apart the houses grew. His neighbors included a
Blazers forward and a Nike VP.

Chance pulled onto the cobblestone driveway, which
encircled a burbling fountain. The house was Tudor-style,
white stucco with half-timbering. It basically looked like
an English cottage on steroids.

"Wow!" Chance whistled. "This place is huge. What does he do again? And is this whole place just for him?"

Milan had always just accepted it as Mr. Kirkby's house, but maybe it was a little too grand to be called something as basic as a house. "In addition to starting Earth Energy, I think he's an investor. And he's divorced and never had any kids."

As Chance parked, Milan unzipped the backpack and took out the pilot's gun. It was heavy and serious, and completely out of place in her mom's Prius.

"Is that a gun?" Chance's voice got higher and thinner.

"I made the mistake of telling Eric that Mom said I should go to Mr. Kirkby." A hot bloom of shame washed over her. "What if the bad guys are here?"

"Whose gun is that?"

"It belonged to the pilot. I found it in his things." She looked over at Chance. "Have you ever shot one?"

He shook his head, eyes wide.

"Me neither."

She had hoped he might have had some experience with firearms. Since he didn't, she leaned forward and slipped it in the back of her waistband. In the last few days, she had seen the dead, tried to comfort the dying, and stared down the barrels of guns just like this one. Confronted with such evil, Chance might initially hesitate. Might not believe whatever was happening was real, at least not in time. But Milan had already learned nightmares can come true.

When she pressed the doorbell a few seconds later, her finger trembled. Was this a mistake?

After a few moments, Mr. Kirkby answered the door. It was a relief to see his familiar steel-rimmed glasses, his dad jeans, his gray hair. He had basically looked the same her whole life.

"Milan!" He put his hand to his heart. "I almost didn't recognize you with your hair cut short. I can't believe it's you!" He put his hands on her shoulders and squeezed for a moment. "And your poor mother, gone." His face creased with concern as he looked her up and down, before his eyes settled back on her face. "What about you? Are you all right? Shouldn't you be in a hospital or something? I know the police have been very—um—concerned about you." He had heard the stories, then.

"I'm actually okay, Mr. Kirkby. But what about you? Because bad people are looking for me. I was worried they might come here."

He raised an eyebrow. It did sound kind of unhinged. At least she had Chance to back her up.

"I'm fine, Milan. And, please, call me Brent. Mr. Kirkby makes me feel like an old man."

"Okay, um, Brent." The word stuck in her throat. "This is my friend Chance."

He nodded, still keeping one hand on the doorframe. "Maybe we should call the police to tell them you're okay so they can call off the search parties. Or have you already talked to them?"

"No." Milan shook her head, missing the feeling of her hair moving. "I'm not sure we can trust them. If we could come in, I'll explain why. My parents found out a secret, and someone's trying to stop it from getting out. And trying to frame me for everything." Did she sound like someone with a loose grasp of reality?

Chance leaned past her. "She's telling the truth, sir. I mean, Brent."

After a moment's hesitation, Brent stepped aside and motioned for them to come in. He led them into the living room, then gestured to the sprawling dark blue sectional. "Please, have a seat."

They took the end closest to the door. He sat on the other, next to an aquarium filled with tropical fish that was built into the wall.

Milan could feel Chance taking in the whole room without being obvious about it. The gleaming hickory-wood floors. The large fireplace, with a TV as big as a queen-size bed mounted above it. The glass-topped mahogany coffee table holding a spray of yellow forsythia. The L-shaped sectional they were sitting on framed a handmade metallic silver and blue rug patterned with intricate designs.

As Brent—it was still hard not to think of him as

Mr. Kirkby—listened intently, Milan filled him in on everything that had happened, starting with the plane crash.

Brent listened, his face betraying nothing. When Milan explained how her mother died, he put his hand over his mouth and closed his eyes for a long moment.

"Your mom was coming to Portland to talk to me. All I know is she wanted to ask my advice." He pushed his glasses back with his thumb. "But I don't know about what. She said she didn't even feel safe talking over the phone."

Milan reached into her pocket and pulled out the thumb drive. "It was about this. It was hidden inside what looked like a car fob on my dad's key ring." She explained how Nikita and Eric and the guy who might be a cop had chased and threatened her, the words tumbling over each other. Chance chimed in whenever she missed a key detail.

Brent's expression sharpened as she explained what was on the drive. He leaned forward and plucked the thumb drive from her hand. "Do you know how much this means?" He held it up. "This draws a clear line between Prospect Power's wells and contamination of the aquifer. This information could lead to regulation of the whole industry. Just a couple of years ago, fracking was banned in four states along the Delaware River because of the risk of water contamination. And that scientist guy actually having those old records from before fracking started—that's the smoking gun."

At the word *gun*, Milan shifted. It felt silly that she still had one tucked in her waistband.

"But why would people do those things if they knew how much damage it could cause?" Chance asked. "There's information on there about people with cancer and babies that died. And so many pictures of dead fish."

"Why does anyone do anything? Money," Brent said simply. "These reserves are worth billions of dollars. People will overlook a lot for that."

Milan thought about how all that money trickled down. "Another thing on the thumb drive is this recording of a threat saying that all the land owners and local businesses were doing great because of fracking."

"Exactly." A muscle flexed in Brent's jaw. "So who else knows about this drive?" He looked at Chance. "Your parents?"

"No. They actually think I'm at school right now. They don't even know Milan was in our house."

Milan leaned forward. "The people who've been hunting me—I don't think they're going to give up."

Brent tilted his head and regarded her. His eyes weren't quite blue, she noticed. They were more a silvery color, like a wolf's. She had known him all her life, but had she ever really paid attention to him?

"Oh, I think you might be right about that."

Emotions were beginning to swirl inside her like a

cyclone. And something else, something black and ugly and sharp, began to take root in her mind.

As he spoke, Brent got to his feet. He opened the glass door to the fireplace. Before Milan or Chance could stop him, before they could even cry out, he tossed the thumb drive into the flames.

As he did, a figure stepped out of the hall. It was the woman Milan had dubbed Nikita.

And in her hand was a gun.

# Chapter 67

## LENNY
# LIKE WE'RE NOT EVEN HERE

"HELLO, MILAN." LENNY KEPT HER VOICE EVEN AS SHE MOVED TO A spot in front of the fireplace. From here, she could see all three exits: the one to the foyer, the one leading deeper into the house, and the windows that overlooked the pool. An exit didn't necessarily mean a door. "Chance." She nodded at him.

The girl lifted her chin and stared defiantly at Lenny. And judging by his expression, the boy was confused about everything except Lenny's gun.

"Get them out of here." Brent waved his now-empty hand. "I can't have their deaths associated with me."

He was like all clients. No matter how big a mess he made, he expected someone else to clean it up. And this one liked his violence at a distance, edited to something he could watch on the big-screen TV behind her. He didn't want it to actually happen in front of him.

"Milan's your goddaughter, Brent," Lenny pointed out. "No one's going to question her choosing to come here, like a poor rabid dog that still has some notion of home. And like a rabid dog, she needed to be put down before she hurt anyone else."

Brent tilted his head, considering this. "And the boy?"

"We can make it look like Milan's the one who shot him. Then you two fought over the gun. And in the struggle, unfortunately she was also shot."

"You can't just talk about us like we're not even here," Milan objected.

Chance put a cautioning hand on Milan's shoulder. He then let it fall to the back of her waist, as if about to pull her close. As Lenny watched, the girl took a half step back. They moved in concert. It was almost like they had practiced this, like they had known that together they would be stronger.

Because when Chance's hand reappeared, it was holding a gun that must have been tucked in Milan's waistband.

Lenny had no idea where the gun had come from. Milan's family hadn't owned one.

But there was no point in wondering where it came from, not when it was already in play.

But rather than point it at Lenny, Chance aimed at

Brent. "You're the one behind all of this, aren't you? Even framing Milan for everything. But why? She said you started Earth Energy and then hired her dad as CEO. Why would you want to cover up how fracking is poisoning the water and making people sick?"

Brent's condescending smile didn't reach his eyes. It barely twisted his lips. "A smart investor diversifies. In other words, you never put all your eggs in one basket. No matter what energy source comes out on top, I'm well positioned. Prospect Power is simply another part of my portfolio. But it's still a sizable percentage."

"Did my dad know?" Milan asked. It was clear she had put her father on a pedestal. Lenny had followed Milan and the boy to the cemetery, seen how the girl fell to her knees in front of his grave marker, bent nearly double. Lenny had gone back to her car to wait and then followed them here.

"When he received the information, he came to me for advice. Of course I didn't tell him how many shares of Prospect Power I held. With Jack, it was never about money or power. It was about a cause." Brent put a sarcastic spin on the word *cause*. "I warned him to leave it alone, but he wouldn't. And worse yet, he wouldn't tell me exactly what he had." He scowled. "Your father had a good heart, but he was also myopic. I mean, what's more important? People being able to put food on their tables? Or a few dead fish?"

Chance made a scoffing noise. "It's not just dead fish

and birds. From what we saw in those lab reports, there's dead people, too. And you killed even more people trying to keep it secret. And now you want to kill Milan and me." His voice cracked slightly in the middle of the last sentence. His hand holding the gun drifted lower.

The boy didn't appear to have the experience or the stomach for actually using a weapon. Then again, Lenny had assumed Milan wasn't capable of half the things she had done. As she considered her best move, a cough scratched its way up from her chest, but she kept her mouth shut and swallowed it back down.

Lenny had never smoked. But it turned out you didn't need to smoke to get lung cancer. You just needed to spend your childhood breathing around someone who did.

Brent shrugged. "You can't make an omelette without breaking eggs. Jack was a genius at seeing how to harness nature's energy: ocean swells, wind, sunlight, rivers. But those sources are hard to transport and store. And fracked gas is making us energy independent right now. In today's world, that's more important than ever."

"And it's making you rich." Chance looked around at the huge room and all its expensive accoutrements. "Richer."

Brett's expression didn't change. "Why don't you put that gun down, son. And then I promise you that Lenny will put hers down, too. We can work something out."

The cough reappeared and pushed back harder, forcing

its way out of Lenny's lips. Red droplets flew through the air and landed on the glass coffee table as well as the rug underneath it.

Brent's face contorted with disgust. "That's a hand-knotted silk rug. It's over two hundred years old!"

Lenny knew firsthand how ugly it would all get. The doctors had drawn fluid from Karl's lungs until they couldn't anymore. Until he was left basically drowning inside his own body. That final day, her father looked like a baby bird fallen from the nest, his bald head wobbling on his weak neck.

After he was gone, no one asked any questions about exactly how he had died. Lenny had just hurried it along a little. At the last moment, he had looked her in the eyes. Fully present. And full of pride.

After this job was done, Lenny had planned to head to Belize, to drink cocktails and let the heat bake her bones. To wait until it felt like it was time to end things for herself.

Only now, standing in front of her client and the children he was paying her to kill, Lenny realized she was not going to clean up Brent's mess.

Not this time.

Instead she was going to make it as big as she could.

# Chapter 68

## MILAN
# SORRY ABOUT THAT

AS BRENT COMPLAINED ABOUT THE BLOOD THAT HAD JUST sprayed from Nikita's mouth, Milan tried to figure out why the woman was bleeding. Had Eric or Bad Cop managed to hurt her before she killed them? But there didn't seem to be a mark on her.

Nikita shrugged. "Sorry about that. You'll want to take care of it before it sets." As she spoke, she put her gun down on the red-flecked glass of the coffee table, between the TV remote and the vase holding the yellow forsythia. She raised her hands theatrically, spreading her fingers to emphasize they were empty. "Put the gun down, Chance. No one has to get hurt here."

Brent didn't take his eyes off Chance's gun. The older

man's body was taut as a coiled spring. Even though she'd been around him dozens, maybe hundreds, of times, Milan realized she'd never actually seen him. Like Little Red Riding Hood, she had focused on the exterior trappings of a familiar, trusted old person instead of seeing the wolf hidden underneath.

Chance cut his eyes to Milan, silently asking what to do. In response, she widened hers, telling him that she didn't know. He hesitated, then set the pilot's gun down. Like Nikita, he took a step back and raised his hands.

As he did, Brent dove for Nikita's gun.

Milan's heart leaped in her chest. She sprang toward the coffee table, her own hands outstretched. She needed to get one of the guns before Brent did.

Nikita drew back her leg and kicked the underside of the coffee table. The glass top flipped over, narrowly missing Milan and Brent, and landed on the rug. All its contents— the two guns, the remote control, the flowers, the vase, and two decorative silver metal birds—went flying. Lenny's gun skittered across the carpet, just out of Milan's reach.

Brent got to it first.

His finger must have tightened on the trigger as he grabbed it, because a shot rang out. Bits of white plaster rained down from the ceiling as the blast echoed off the floor, walls, and windows. The shock of it stole Milan's breath. Lenny was the only one who didn't flinch. Instead she was doubled over, one hand pulling up her pant leg.

Taking aim at Milan, Brent got up on his other elbow, then a hand, and then to his feet. The gun never wavered from its focus on her heart.

"I'm sorry, dear," Brent said, "but you've left me no choice."

*BANG! BANG!*

In quick succession, two silvery dimples appeared in the huge black screen of the TV behind him.

Using the small gun she had just pulled from a holster strapped to her calf, Nikita had shot the TV. She pivoted. *BANG!* The aquarium exploded. As Brent let out a wordless wail of protest, a waterfall filled with flopping neon fish poured out.

"Oops," Nikita said, deadpan. "Looks like I got some on the rug."

"What are you doing?" Brent's face was a mask of anger.

"I'm letting you know this has gone far enough." Despite everything, no emotion colored her voice.

His eyes narrowed. "I think you're forgetting who is paying who."

"Whom," she corrected.

"Whatever. One of us has to finish this thing. Tie up these last loose ends." With his chin, he indicated Milan and Chance. "And if it's not you, then it's going to be me."

Milan had automatically taken a step back when Brent aimed the gun at her. Now she spotted a metallic gleam underneath the sectional. The pilot's gun? Quick as a thought, she dropped to her knees and grabbed for it.

"Get up, Milan!" Brent ordered. He probably didn't want to shoot her in the back. It wouldn't fit with the story he was trying to construct.

Instead of a gun, it was one of the silver metal birds. Milan half turned and threw it at Brent. It sailed past his head but still made him flinch and step back. Chance was half-crouched, his fists clenched, his eyes jumping from person to person. Milan reached farther back under the couch, surfing her hand over the wet floor, but found nothing.

"I told you to get up," Brent said. "You need to listen when I talk."

And then he swiveled and shot Chance.

"No!" Milan screamed.

Everything seemed to slow down.

With a groan, Chance clapped his hands to the left side of his chest. He sat down heavily on the sectional and then doubled over. Blood began to drip between his fingers and onto the wet floor.

Then Milan spotted it. Behind Chance's feet, tucked under the sectional, was the pilot's gun. Scrabbling forward, she leaned into Chance's leg as she grabbed it. Unlike when she had first held it, now it seemed to belong in her hand. The gun led the way as, blood roaring in her ears, vision blurring, she turned to face Brent. She got to her feet, the gun never wavering from his chest. She steadied her right hand with her left. Both were shaking, but not because she was afraid to pull the trigger. It was because she wanted to do it so badly. She wanted to hurt Brent. She wanted to kill him. She wanted to make it so that he had never been born.

His gun was also once again aimed at her chest. But Milan no longer had a heart.

"You're not going to shoot me, Milan," he said.

She didn't bother to answer.

"You won't do it," he said confidently. "I've known you since you were a baby. You're not a killer."

"I will," Milan said, gripping the gun even more tightly. "I swear I will." But she could feel his words getting under her skin.

"He's right, Milan," Nikita said. "You don't want to do this."

"Oh, yes I do," Milan retorted. "I very much want to do this." Her voice was full of tears, and she cursed herself for showing emotion. "He's taken everything I had." On her wrist, next to the butt of the gun, were those letters she had so painfully made, dot by dot, just a few months ago. WWJD? *What Would Jack Do?*

What would her dad do? Would he really shoot his old mentor? Or would he hesitate?

But her dad wasn't here. And Milan was. And her life was on the line.

*Hell yes.*

She pulled the trigger.

# Chapter 69

## LENNY
# WHITE LIGHT OR UTTER BLACKNESS

LENNY SAW A DOZEN MICROEXPRESSIONS FLICKER ACROSS THE girl's face as she leveled the pistol at Brent. Because that's what Milan was in the end. A girl. Trained or not, she was still a girl.

One who had never done this before. And who would be forever changed once she did.

Milan's expression morphed into something that was a cross between rage and terror. Just as the girl pulled the trigger, Lenny pushed Brent out of the way.

When the bullet hit her torso, she grunted. It felt like a huge iron fist had punched all the way through. Her momentum carried both her and Brent to the floor, with her on top. But the red on his shirt, Lenny realized, was all hers.

"You saved me," Brent gasped. His glasses were pushed up on one side.

"I wasn't saving you." Lenny twisted the gun from his hand, hard enough that he yelped. "I was saving Milan from having to live with herself. She's just a kid."

And then she shot him.

For a second, Brent struggled, his legs kicking weakly. But then his head fell back and his body went limp.

Lenny didn't think she was capable of moving. She knew what happened when a high-velocity projectile impacted solid and semi-solid objects. The proof was under her. The proof was inside her. Things were starting to feel fuzzy around the edges.

For a second, she waited. For the white light. Or utter blackness. For the feeling of her soul lifting or Karl's hand reaching out to take hers.

But nothing happened.

"Chance!"

At the sound of Milan's anguished cry, Lenny tried to turn over, but her legs didn't seem to work anymore. She settled for turning her head.

The boy was slumped sideways on the sectional. The blue fabric was stained with an ever-widening dark circle. Milan was shaking his shoulder. He didn't answer or even move. She yanked his phone from his rear pocket and tapped on it. The room was quiet enough that Lenny could hear the person on the other end answer.

"911. What is your emergency?"

"There's been a shooting. A lot of them. I think my friend might be dying."

"And you're at—" The woman read out Brent's address. When Milan agreed, the dispatcher said in a calm voice, "We're dispatching an ambulance and the police right now."

"Milan!" Lenny had to repeat her name several times to get her attention. "Milan! You need to put direct pressure on the wound now."

The girl's eyes were so wide Lenny could see white on either side.

"Yours?"

She gave Milan her best approximation of a smile. How had she ever thought the girl was trained?

"No. Chance's. It's a little late for me." The burning sensation in her abdomen was spreading. She paused to gather her breath. "Get him on the floor, interlace your fingers, and put the palm of your bottom hand flat over the wound. Keep your arms straight, with your shoulders directly over it. Put as much weight as you can on it to compress the blood vessels."

Milan got her hands in Chance's armpits and followed instructions, wincing as she dragged him to the floor and then pressed on the wound. "That's right," Lenny said softly. "You're doing it right." The edges of her vision were fading, and what was left seemed to be receding.

"What about Mr. Kirkby?" Milan asked.

"He's dead."

The girl started to cry, tears dripping onto Chance's face.

Chance's eyes fluttered open.

"Milan?"

"I'm right here," she said. "I'm not going anyplace."

And that was how the police found them when they came busting in the front door.

As they did, Lenny let go of whatever was still holding her on earth.

# Chapter 70

## JANIE

# WE GOT THEM

JANIE HAD FINALLY TRACKED DOWN FLOYD HIGGINS AT THE assisted-living facility where he now lived. She'd been horrified to read about his injuries and doubted that they were accidental.

She peeked in the room the attendant had pointed out to her. He was sitting in an old wheelchair with the feet paddles folded out of the way, his head hanging low. When he saw her, he started to shuffle his feet to bring himself closer. Looking at him, his shoulders hunched over, his body shrunken, Janie wanted to weep. But then he tilted his face up to her and she saw that his eyes were as alive as ever.

"We got them, Floyd. Thanks to your information."

When he'd heard rumors that fracking companies were

sniffing around, Floyd had had the foresight to gather water samples from all the places he had liked to fish. Many of those streams and lakes had ended up being contaminated by PFAS used to make fracking more efficient.

Janie held up the newspaper with the front-page story about Prospect Power being fined twelve million dollars by the state's Environmental Protection Agency. Criminal charges had been filed against all their higher-ups. These turned out to include Steve Hamill, despite his aw-shucks demeanor. Still, one night she had gotten a call from a number with no caller ID. The person on the other end had choked out, "I'm so sorry." And she was pretty sure it had been Steve.

After reading him the article, she lifted her head. "And that's just the beginning. Your old lab has been charged with committing fraud and conspiracy by accepting bribes to manipulate test results after you were hurt. The state's going to ban the use of PFAS for fracking, and other states are looking at the same legislation. And there's a class action suit. It's going to take some time, but we're going to get justice." Janie sighed, thinking of things that could never be put right. "Or at least as much justice as we can get."

Floyd's eyes rolled. He groaned.

No. It was more than just a groan. He was trying to say something. Janie leaned closer.

"Thank God."

# Chapter 71

## MILAN

# MAKE A WISH

### Four months later

MILAN AND CHANCE LAY SIDE BY SIDE ON AN OLD GRAY WOOL blanket, looking up at the diamond-like stars scattered over the black velvet sky. It was just after midnight. They had spread their blanket in the center of the large grassy oval that capped Mt. Tabor Park. Even though there were dozens of people around them, the darkness made it feel like they were alone.

With a clear sky and only a thin sliver of the new moon, conditions were perfect for watching the Perseid meteor shower. Once or twice a minute, a shooting star arced across the sky. Some were delicate wisps while others blazed with a fiery intensity.

As a particularly long-lasting white streak arced above them, Chance gasped.

Hearing that intake of air, Milan flashed back again to how still Chance had been after Brent shot him. But thanks to the advice from the woman she had dubbed Nikita, Milan had been able to stop the bleeding. The bullet had missed a lot of important things but still damaged a nerve in his left arm. Physical therapy was helping him regain range of motion. Some days Milan felt proud for how she had been able to save him. Other days she felt guilty, thinking he had only been hurt because of her.

It had taken the police several weeks to identify Nikita's real name: Lena. The daughter of a criminal, Lena had been a one-woman wrecking crew for Brent, doing anything to keep Prospect Power's crimes a secret. She had been identified by Floyd Higgins, the water scientist, as the one who had pushed him down his basement stairs and then whispered a warning in his ear before she left.

Lena's autopsy had also revealed that she had terminal lung cancer. Was that why she had taken the bullet meant for Brent?

An orange streak blazed across the heavens, followed by a bright green in a different corner of the sky. Milan's dad had taught her that the cool thing about a meteor shower was that you didn't need binoculars or a telescope. All you had to do was lie back, let your eyes adjust to the darkness, and try to take in as much of the sky as possible.

Milan thought she might never fully take in everything that had happened four months earlier. Lena had saved her and had helped her save Chance, but she had also killed so many, including Milan's parents and Eric. Eric, who had used his paychecks, then credit card advances, and finally senatorial office funds to make illegal—and losing—bets on sports.

Brent Kirkby, another of Lena's victims, was a little easier to understand. Despite what her dad had thought, Brent had always been motivated by money, not saving the planet. First, the rising cost of fuel had led him to found Earth Energy. When fracking offered a new way to more cheaply wring oil and gas from the earth, Brent had become the majority shareholder in Prospect Power.

Two more meteors, one pink and one orange, sliced across the sky in quick succession, drawing murmurs of appreciation from the unseen people around them.

Milan's dad had told her that most meteors were only as big as a grain of sand. Yet they made so much light they could awe hundreds of people.

In the same vein, the tiny thumb drive continued to make huge waves. Brent had tossed it in the fire, thinking he was destroying the evidence. But before leaving Chance's house, Milan had made a copy. She had buried it, wrapped in a plastic baggie, in the loose dirt next to her dad's grave marker. If she hadn't lived to retrieve it, Milan had hoped whoever dug her mother's grave might find it.

A small dairy farmer who had supplied some of the information on the thumb drive, Janie, was now the lead plaintiff in a class action lawsuit against Prospect Power. The company had vowed to fight, but the lab reports, photos, and medical records were damning. Not only had Prospect been fined by the state's Department of Environmental Protection, but it was being investigated for environmental crimes.

Milan found herself shivering, not from the chill in the air, but from the thought of just how close Prospect had come to concealing its wrongdoing.

Chance put his arm around her shoulder and pulled her close. "Getting cold?" he murmured into her ear.

The warmth of his breath made a different kind of shiver run through her. Were they still just friends and neighbors? People who had helped each other survive, despite the odds? Or could they be more than that? She had only been back in Portland for a few weeks, and in another two she would be gone. Back to Colorado, where she would start her senior year at Briar Woods.

Ms. Robbins had reached out to Milan as soon as she heard about the accident. Their texts and calls had grown more frequent while Milan's relatives tried to figure out what to do with her. For the first two months, she'd lived with her mom's mom in a small town in Montana. But her grandma was seventy-eight and the two of them had little in common besides having both loved her mom.

Her dad's parents had also offered to have her come live with them, as had an uncle and an aunt. But, for various reasons, no one seemed a good fit. Milan had many conversations with Ms. Robbins about what to do. They had also discussed the improvements the headmistress was making to Briar Woods Academy. The first had been encouraging the literature teacher to retire. The second was planning a unit that would focus on fracking.

Eventually, Milan had asked her relatives if she could spend her last year of high school at Briar Woods.

Overhead, a neon-green meteor changed to a purple color as it flew. Its brilliance seemed to last for several seconds. All around them were gasps of delight.

Chance pulled her closer. "Make a wish," he whispered.

Closing her eyes, Milan did.

# ACKNOWLEDGMENTS

ONE OF MY FAVORITE THINGS ABOUT WRITING IS THAT I GET TO DO deep dives into topics I might not otherwise think about.

Scott Gratsinger (my newfound second cousin's brother) answered my very newbie questions about private planes.

Eric Hill, an experienced aviator (and who is absolutely not related to the Eric in this book), helped me devise a scheme to take down a plane and even sent me recordings of the various cockpit alarms.

Mike Blackburn, a drone hobbyist, helped me brainstorm an interesting twist.

Paul Holmquist, director of customer support at Raisbeck Engineering, answered my very strange questions about the overwing lockers they manufacture—including sharing that the door weighs just five pounds.

Survival expert Mike Pewtherer helped me brainstorm how Milan could survive her trip down an icy mountain. He's the author of *Wilderness Survival: Living Off the Land with the*

*Clothes on Your Back and the Knife on Your Belt* and *Wilderness Survival Handbook: Primitive Skills for Short-Term Survival and Long-Term Comfort*, both of which were very helpful.

As a writer, I have done many things for research, but probably the most intense was a three-day course called Urban Escape and Evasion. The final day of class, you are "kidnapped": hooded, cuffed, and mouth duct-taped. Then you are taken somewhere dark and uncomfortable. You must use all your newly learned skills to escape, and then accomplish a series of tasks, like picking a lock or getting a stranger to give you a ride. All the while, expert trackers are hunting you down. That class has proved endlessly useful, most especially for this book.

Garrett Lehman, who works in the renewable energy industry, helped me better understand fracking, the regulations affecting it, and how the industry does not have to disclose what chemicals it injects deep underground.

Erica Jackson, manager of Community Outreach and Support at FracTracker.org, answered my numerous questions about fracking and how it affects the environment.

Hydrogeologist Bob Brinkmann at the Oregon Department of Geology and Mineral Industries patiently answered my questions about the possibility of fracking in Oregon.

Even though the geology of Oregon precludes most fracking, fracking has still affected the state. From 2016 to 2019, two million pounds of radioactive fracking waste—highly contaminated filters, tank sludge, and slurry from drilling pipes—were transported to Oregon on unmarked railcars and illegally buried in a landfill near the Columbia River. On average, the waste registered radium at thirty times the state's limit, with some waste at three hundred times the limit.

PFAS, also known as "forever chemicals," refers to more than twelve thousand chemicals that persist in the environment and can build up in the body. They are widely used in industry and consumer products, ranging from clothing and cosmetics to fast-food wrappers and microwave popcorn bags. A new study from the United States Geological Survey (USGS) estimates that these contaminants taint nearly half the nation's tap water.

A hydrologist who works for the USGS and who did not want to be publicly acknowledged helped me write more accurately about PFAS.

Chance Diaz not only teaches me Brazilian jujitsu but also let me borrow his name.

With *Stay Dead*, Christy Ottaviano has once again worked her editorial magic. This is our fifteenth book together, and my thirtieth with my agent, Wendy Schmalz. I love working with strong women who are committed to making each book as good as it can be.

The entire team at my publisher is awesome, from the strong leadership to the thoughtful planning of marketing, publicity, design, production, sales, and more. Megan Tingley, president and publisher of Little, Brown Books for Young Readers, sets the tone from the very top. Victoria Stapleton, executive director of School and Library marketing, gets right to the heart of why I write. Christie Michel, manager of School and Library marketing, has helped untangle me more than once. Publicists Cheryl Lew and Kelly Moran help bring my books to people's attention, as well as making sure I get from place to place. Additional thanks go to Leyla Erkan, Marisa Finkelstein, Bill Grace, Emilie Polster, and Jackie Engel. Neil Swaab designed the beautiful cover.

My booking agent, Carmen Oliver, is worth her weight in books. With her assistance, I am able to speak to thousands of students each year.

*Randy Patten*

# APRIL HENRY

is the *New York Times* bestselling author of many acclaimed mysteries for adults and over fifteen novels for teens, including the bestselling *Girl, Stolen*; *Girl Forgotten*, which was a Junior Library Guild Gold Standard Selection and a Tome Student Literacy Society It List Selection; *Two Truths and a Lie*, which was a Junior Library Guild Gold Standard Selection and a YALSA Top Ten Quick Pick for Reluctant Young Adult Readers; and *The Girl I Used to Be*, which was nominated for an Edgar Award and won the Anthony Award for Best YA Mystery. She lives in Oregon and invites you to visit her at aprilhenry.com.